The Persevering Woman

M.L. Lexi

BOOK TWO OF THE DETERMINED WOMAN SERIES

Titles by M.L. Lexi

The Blind Woman
The Deceitful Woman
The Forgiving Woman
The Grieving Woman
The Guilty Woman
The Loyal Woman
The Noble Woman
The Resolute Woman
The Unfaithful Woman

The Farfalla Family Saga

The Determined Woman
The Persevering Woman
The Invincible Woman

The Fearless Woman Series

The Fearless Woman
The Naïve Woman

Copyright

To persevering mothers and the daughters they foster.

Nothing changes, but for what has to.

—M.L. Lexi

Prologue

THE PROCESSION OF cars following the black hearse into St. Paul's Presbyterian Cemetery was thirty long. Slowly, the cars made their way through the cemetery to Mrs. Emily Johnstone's final resting place. A few minutes in, the hearse stopped before the mausoleum Isabella had built for Mrs. Johnstone's last resting place.

The mausoleum, constructed of white marble, stood tall amongst the headstones jutting from the snow-covered ground. Above the entrance door, a hand-carved angel strummed a gold lyre. On opposite sides of the door, colourful orchids speared from tall white urns. It was a grand structure, but Isabella Farfalla believed it was what Mrs. Johnstone deserved.

Mrs. Johnstone was much more to Isabella than the bank manager, who decades ago gave a young, naïve girl the opportunity of a lifetime. Emily Johnstone was a friend and mentor. Because of Emily Johnstone, Isabella owned and managed the worldwide renowned billion-dollar Isabella Farfalla Fashion empire.

Because of Mrs. Johnstone, the fashion-conscious sought Isabella's designer clothes, handbags, shoes, accessories, and perfumes. Mrs. Johnstone's foresight had made it possible for celebrities, the elite, and royalty to want to be seen in Isabella Farfalla's original design. Isabella's elegant, graceful designs had walked down the red carpet, appeared on various theatrical stages, and worn at galas, Hollywood award shows, first ladies, and royalty. Isabella's designs and gold butterfly logo were as recognizable as Gucci's interlocked "G" s and Chanel's bold interlaced "C" s.

As much as Isabella's husband, Antonio Sabatini, and Sal Mesi, her biological father—who appeared in her life decades later—ultimately had a hand in her success, Emily Johnstone believed in Isabella enough to approve the loan that helped launch her company.

Opening the car door, Isabella stepped out. The air was crisp, and cooler air prevailed, but the drizzle of snow that fell melted under the late morning's bright sun.

Filling her lungs with air, Isabella raised the collar of her coat. Her long, glossy mink hair was a dark contrast against the cream-coloured mohair coat. She wore black knee-high boots with a high spiked heel and pointed toes. Isabella's brown, red-rimmed hazel eyes were shaded behind dark Farfalla sunglasses. At sixty-five, her olive skin remained mainly untouched by the many hardships she'd faced. Maybe more than most had dealt with, but perseverance made Isabella come out a survivor in the end.

Closed doors led to open ones was Isabella's philosophy. That creed helped Isabella overcome homelessness after her father's death at the unfair young age of forty-one left her with mounting bills. Isabella's philosophy helped her survive bankruptcy, betrayal, blackmail, and the stalker who ultimately traumatized her and stole her dignity and life.

For twenty-one difficult years, Isabella doubted her daughter's origin, and the doubt remained at the heart of her marriage for as long. Keeping the secret internalized and keeping it from Antonio, her husband, was the hardest thing Isabella had done.

When the truth emerged twenty-one years into their marriage, Antonio declined to read the DNA report and unquestioningly accepted Bianca as his daughter. Antonio stuck by Isabella then, and four decades later, he was still by her side, his love for her as ardent as ever.

Closing the car door behind him, Antonio reached for Isabella's hand and held it tight. Isabella looked over at him. He'd aged like a fine Italian wine. Hovering on his seventieth birthday, he was still as handsome as when she met him.

Antonio's hair, dashingly grayed at the temples, crowned the handsome face with the sea-blue eyes she fell in love with. He wore a navy tweed coat over a black silk suit with a white shirt, burgundy tie, and brown Mesi derby shoes. Isabella smiled. As striking as he looked, Antonio was never comfortable out of his customary jeans and a cotton shirt with the sleeves rolled to the elbows.

After Antonio successfully launched The Café franchise across Canada, Isabella tried to talk him out of the cotton shirt and jeans and into a more professional look. Isabella failed miserably and just as well because she did not mind admiring the six-three-frame fit in those snug jeans.

"Are you all right?" Antonio reached for Isabella's hand and held it tightly.

"I already miss her," Isabella said softly. "It feels as if it's the end of an era."

"Yes, but in all fairness, and no disrespect to Emily, she was ninety-two," said Antonio.

"Dad's ninety-three, and Mama's not far behind." Isabella watched Bianca and Lorenzo attempt to corral their daughters, Rosanna, ten and Serena, seven, from running off when they exited their car with little success.

"Youthful energy," Antonio sighed with a smile. "Your father and mother, *amore*, much like Emily, are a force to be reckoned with. For God's sake, Emily outlived three husbands. As for your parents, they still have enough energy to keep up with those two girls and all their great-grandchildren."

"Are you going to leave the girls lying in the snow?" Isabella said to her daughter on her approach. Bianca wore a gray coat, tapered black pants and laced-up ankle boots.

"They'll get tired soon enough and join us." Bianca shouldered her handbag, brushed the chestnut hair that tumbled in waves around her face and straightened the sunglasses, shading the blue eyes so much like her father's. "Lorenzo will deal with them. He has the patience of a sloth."

We do marry our parents, Isabella thought, watching Lorenzo patiently handle the girl as Antonio would.

"But never mind the girls, Mom. Are you all right? You weren't doing well at the church."

Isabella brought her hand to Bianca's cheek. "I'm fine, honey. Cold, but fine."

Bianca watched her father's arm tighten around her mother's waist in a circle of comfort and warmth. Here was love, Bianca thought. Her father would move mountains for her mother if she asked him. Bianca hoped she and Lorenzo would be as in love and devoted to one another after decades of marriage as her parents were.

"She was such a lovely woman—tough as nails but lovely. She taught me loads. I will miss Mrs. Johnstone, and the girls will miss their second Nana." Bianca turned to watch her girls lay down on the snow to make snow angels while Lorenzo watched on. "Christ, I have to put a stop to this. They're getting their coats wet and dirty."

Isabella caught Bianca's arm before she turned to go. "Leave them, honey. Emily wouldn't mind one bit. If anything, she'd encourage the laughter and fun they're having, as her family does. See what I mean?"

Bianca, Antonio, and Isabella watched Mrs. Johnstone's gaggle of great-great-grandchildren, encouraged by their parents, lay down next to Rosanna and Serena with them watching on.

Over the giggles and laughter of the children making snow angels, Christian walked up and did precisely what

Isabella predicted of her thirty-eight-year-old son. He lay next to Rosanna and Serena in the snow.

Bianca's slash of dark eyebrows rose. "He needs to get himself a wife."

Isabella nodded. "Yes, he does." Isabella looked at Antonio then. His eyes were bright and smiling. "You need to speak to him."

"Yeah. Sure. I will." Antonio agreed when Isabella narrowed her eyes. "Your parents are here," he said to change the conversation.

Isabella waved Salvatore and Maria over. "Let's get to it. Bianca, honey, round the troops and have everyone head to the mausoleum. Emily was a stickler for punctuality in life, and we're not about to start to disappoint her now."

THERE WERE SO MANY PEOPLE THERE. It was easy for an outsider to blend into the group, but she stayed well behind. Some of those in attendance flew in from around the world to attend Emily Johnstone's funeral. Unlike what she'd been told, Emily Johnstone wasn't a hated woman. Emily Johnstone was very much loved.

Blue Eyes scanned the group. Isabella and her clan, the Sabatinis and the Mesis, were there. It was rumoured Isabella paid fifty thousand dollars to build the mausoleum where the stiff was to be buried.

Blue Eyes hated rich people. Blue Eyes' fingers lightly tapped the tree as if striking piano keys to deal with the mounting resentment eating her insides.

Blue Eyes saw the famous runway model Kat LeBlanc, now Kat LeBlanc-Mesi, who, thanks to Isabella, went from working as a receptionist for Emily Johnstone to the runway. From there, it was a matter of time before Kat got her hooks into Isabella's bastard brother, Carlo Mesi, and became one of the wealthiest women in Europe.

Kat risked her perfect modelling figure to give Carlo the twin sons to carry his legacy. It was a paltry gesture for what she got in return, thought Blue Eyes.

Blue Eyes saw the old man, Salvatore Mesi, Isabella's biological father, who had started the company Carlo had taken over. His wife Maria, Isabella's biological mother, whom Salvatore left knocked up, stood by him. The only reason Blue Eyes could think of for the old woman to take Salvatore back after abandoning her when she was pregnant with Isabella had to be for his money. What respectable woman takes back a man who disappears overnight and reappears decades later?

Blue Eyes flicked her attention to Christian when he approached the hunky Lorenzo Romano. Lorenzo wasn't just an excellent designer, but he was a whole lot of gorgeous. Blue Eyes was sure she could fulfill his wildest fantasies in bed better than his pretentious, haughty wife Bianca could. Blue Eyes let her mind wander for fifteen seconds before forcing herself to focus. Christian was the man she'd flown across an ocean to meet, not Lorenzo.

The long, dark curls, the broad shoulders, the fashionable stubble, and those blue eyes had her swooning. Christian looked better in person than in the photographs she had seen on tabloid covers and pages. She could see why he was labelled the most desirable bachelor.

Sexy good looks were a plus, but that didn't interest her as much as his bank account. Christian Sabatini was worth millions, and that very much interested her.

Part I

The Beginning

The only remedy is to tackle the problem head-on.

—M.L. Lexi

Chapter 1

THE WEIGHT OF Bianca's shock palpable, Isabella waited while her daughter processed what she'd said.

Bianca's hair, pulled back in a French twist with strands framing her face, underscored the large blue eyes and full lips. Her skin had the look of outdoor colour, and she wore muted makeup. She had on a lilac dress with a wide skirt and thick waist. The black stilettos added four inches to her five-five height. There was a white gold chain around her neck from which an enviable diamond hung. At her ears, she wore studs and on her left hand was the white gold wedding band with a blindingly large sapphire.

"Me? CEO?" Bianca's voice was barely a whisper as if she were afraid to speak the words aloud and make them unreal.

Like her mother, Bianca was the essence of grace and elegance. But then Bianca had spent her entire life rooted in the fashion industry and learned everything there was to know about style from the best—her mother.

Isabella and Antonio watched their dumbfounded daughter rise from the sofa in one fluid motion. On rubbery legs, in stunned silence, Bianca paced the shiny marble floor veined with gray to the fireplace fashioned out of the same stone.

The living room was scented by the scent of pine from the Christmas tree her mother traditionally left standing until the first week of January, along with the burning maple logs from the fireplace. Two large red poinsettias sat on the console table behind the long, mustard-coloured sofa.

Walls were washed in shades of blood orange and tangerine. A collection of family portraits hung on one wall. Artifacts and eclectic art from Isabella's and Antonio's worldwide travels sat on white lacquer shelves and pedestals. Through the tall double-plated glass wall, you could see the roll of land surrounding their home, now blanketed in white snow. A floating moon on the horizon shadowed the grove of pines surrounding the estate.

Bianca grabbed a maple log from the stack next to the fireplace and tossed it into the fading fire. The crackle of flame and wood filled the thunderous silence in the room.

Since Bianca was a girl, she'd dreamed of this moment. She pushed herself to excel in school to get here. She studied marketing, design, and management to prove her worth to her mother, who, in Bianca's eyes, naturally excelled at everything.

And Bianca didn't oppose her mother when she insisted she work her way from the ground up as everyone else had to at her company. Bianca did it because she believed learning every aspect of the company would make her a better leader when she stepped into her mother's giant shoes. But as much as Bianca hoped for this day to come, for as long as she'd prepared for it, the shock struck her like a hand grenade to her system.

When she turned to face her mother sitting on the sofa beside Antonio, Bianca stared at her. Impeccably dressed as Isabella always was, she looked smart in the red dress that hugged her slim body. Unlike her fashionable mother, her father opted for simplicity over fashion and wore faded jeans and a white shirt. Both sipped whiskey from the baccarat lowball glass Christian poured for them.

Bianca started to open her mouth but closed it again and sat when Isabella motioned her to the chair next to Lorenzo.

"As I was saying, your father and I would like you to take over the company's operation," Isabella said.

That brought on a longer, more stunned silence.

Bianca levelled her gaze on Isabella. "The entire Isabella Farfalla Fashion Company?" Bianca replied, her voice laced with a tremor of emotion.

"Yes. You'll be in charge of the operation of the local manufacturing, the overseas factories, and the global stores." Isabella waved her empty glass at Christian, who took it from her and moved to refresh her drink. "You will also take over the supervision of the head office here in Toronto and the satellite offices in New York, London, and Paris."

Bianca flicked baffled eyes to Lorenzo sitting beside her in the button-tufted, plush chair with a smile on his face.

"Do you know what you're saying, Mom? You said you'd only retire when you were six feet under. Is this an emotional reaction to Mrs. Johnstone's funeral? It's been only a day since we buried her," Bianca said after swallowing the glass of brandy Christian handed her.

Isabella's slash of dark eyebrows rose. "When have you known me to make rash decisions, especially concerning my business? Your father and I have been discussing this for months. You've been preparing for this moment your entire life, Bianca. You have the passion, the knowledge, and the determination to lead this company into the future. I believe you're ready. The question is, are you up to it?" Isabella's gaze remained steady on her daughter.

Lorenzo squeezed Bianca's hand, a silent gesture of support and unwavering belief. "You were born for this, amore," he murmured, his dark eyes filled with admiration.

The spark that ignited in Bianca's eyes replaced the initial shock with a surge of determination she jumped in to say, "I was, wasn't I? Yes. Yes. Yes, I'm ready for this, Mom."

"Your mother said you would be, and she's never wrong," Antonio said. "I'm turning seventy soon."

"That's not for two years, Daddy."

Antonio continued. "Time is passing us by quickly, and seventy will come sooner than later. I want to slow down—some. I've been working since my teens, and it's time to step back. I've already set my exit plan in motion. A press release will be made in the coming week announcing the sale of The Café."

"To the Brazilian conglomerate. Christian said you and him finalized the deal to sell your company to them." Bianca held her glass out to Christian as he sat down.

"What am I, the bartender around here? Just because you're two years older doesn't give you the right to boss me around." Christian was the spitting image of his father, but jeans and a white cotton shirt weren't his style. Christian wore a blue cashmere sweater over a silk burgundy shirt and black pleated gabardine pants. His hair was trimmed, as was the dark stubble around the square jaw.

"Shut up and pour," Bianca ordered with the tone of an older sister.

Isabella rolled her eyes. "Children, please. You'd think you weren't adults."

"I will pour it for you, amore." Lorenzo pushed to his feet and walked the brandy and whiskey bottle on the console table to the sitting area in his typically calm demeanour.

Lorenzo wore tapered jeans, a buttoned-down black shirt with the sleeves halfway rolled up, and black loafers. His thick wave of curls hung to his shoulders and was as dark as his forever-smiling eyes. His stubble was neatly trimmed.

Following Lorenzo with her eyes as he topped everyone's glass, Isabella thought he was so much like Antonio at his age. In addition to his handsome good looks, Lorenzo was a calm bastion of nerves, unlike Bianca, who was wired very much like she was. Bianca was high-strung and restless. As Bianca's opposite, Lorenzo was what she needed in her life to keep her calm and grounded.

"Drink it, amore. It will calm you." Lorenzo's voice flowed musically with the Italian inflection that never left him after years of living in Toronto.

"Do as your husband says, Bianca. He knows best," Isabella commented, giving Lorenzo a wink as he topped Bianca's glass.

"As I was saying," Antonio interjected. "The sale of The Café will be announced next week, and the deal will close by year's end. That will free a lot of my time to do what I should be doing at my age."

"And what's that, Daddy?" Bianca sent the brandy streaming down her throat.

"Traveling for pleasure, not business, and enjoying the properties your mother and I have acquired around the world throughout our hardworking life, which to date we have had little chance to enjoy." Antonio flashed sharp blue eyes at Isabella before he reached for her hand. "And I'd like to do it with your mother, so she needs to free up her time by handing the reigns to you, Bianca."

"Out of the fifteen hundred The Café stores, we're keeping one hundred—the maximum the Brazilian's allowed. We will manage them until Rosanna and Serena turn twenty-five when each will receive twenty-five stores. And...." Christian paused momentarily, "My children each will get twenty-five."

Bianca lifted a single dark eyebrow. "Well, you have pollinated half of the earth's female population. I'm sure you can dig up two kids from somewhere."

Antonio and Lorenzo hooted a laugh while Isabella sighed and cast her eyes to the heavens. "Stop it, you two. Christian will marry and produce grandchildren. Won't you, honey?"

"If I must." Christian aimed his eyes beyond the glass wall.

The snow was coming down in a thick sheet of white. Tree branches were heavy with it, and under a full moon, the land was shrouded in a silvery haze. In the distance, Christian thought he saw a couple of deer foraging for their dinner.

"You must. Honey, you're thirty-eight, and it's time to settle down. After years of bachelorhood, even George Clooney realized the error of his ways and settled down to make a family. Your father and I aren't getting any younger, and I don't want to leave this earth with the worry that you'll be alone."

"Christ, Mom, you have many years yet, and you know there are a lot of benefits to being single. I don't have to put up with women like her." Christian jutted his chin at his sister Bianca and then turned to Lorenzo. "I salute your resilience, brother-in-law. You, my man, are made of steel." Christian lifted his glass in a half-salute.

A wise man, Lorenzo neither acknowledged nor reacted to Christian's comment.

"There are a lot of benefits to sharing your life with someone who's always by your side and who shares your dreams. Someone you can talk to about anything, a life partner who believes in everything you do and is there to pick you up when you're down." Antonio closed a hand over Isabella's.

"Et tu, Brutus. What happened to male solidarity, Dad?" Christian took a long pull of his whiskey.

"Son, like Lorenzo, I know better than to turn against my wife." Antonio gave Lorenzo a side-eye look. "Nodding, smiling, and listening are techniques you might consider polishing. If you were married, you'd know that."

Isabella patted Antonio's hand. "That, amore, is the perfect answer." Isabella turned her eyes to her son. "Christian, promise me you'll at least consider settling down."

"I will, Mom." Christian leaned in to peck Isabella on the cheek. "Now, why don't you finish telling Bianca your plan? I'm sure she's anxious to know about her new role, which I one hundred percent approve." Christian slanted a look over Isabella's shoulder at his father and winked.

"All right, let's move on," Isabella said, and Antonio's mouth tipped up at the corners at his crafty son. Shifting the conversation was a refined skill Christian had employed with proficiency since childhood. The boy was, without a doubt, his son. "I'd like Lorenzo to assume the fashion designer and creative director role for Farfalla's."

"I cannot do that, Isabella. You are Farfalla's the brand and the designer everyone wants."

"You can and will. Honey, you're as good as me, maybe better. I'll deny that outside of this room."

"I do not believe that, and you do not have to deny it because it is not the truth. You have taught me everything I know." Lorenzo's words, tinged with sincerity, made Isabella choke.

Isabella reached for Lorenzo's hand. "Honey, you're like a son to me, and I want no one for the job but you. Make me proud."

Lorenzo's eyes filled with emotion, and shrugging in resignation said, "I will try my best, Isabella. Thank you for the opportunity."

"With you as my fashion designer, Bianca as the CEO, and Christian as the CFO, Antonio and I leave the company in good hands. Don't we, honey?" Isabella turned to Antonio, who nodded in tacit agreement.

"You do, Mom. I promise we'll make you proud. I'll make you proud." Bianca threw her arms around her mother. "I will ensure the company continues to be your legacy, and we'll make it as successful as you have for future generations."

"It's all I ask, baby," Isabella said.

The emotional moment between the mother and daughter was interrupted by the arrival of Romeo, a white-coated Maltese with round, dark eyes and floppy ears, who barked as he ran into the room. Rosanna chased after him while Serena casually strolled behind her sister.

Both girls wore plaid pinafores with a white turtleneck sweater and black tights. They had a curly spill of chestnut hair around their faces with blue eyes. At one year, Serena's senior, Rosanna, was inches taller and had inherited her mother's rambunctious personality. Serena was her father's daughter, and mellow was her nature.

"Nana says, 'everyone to the table. Dinner's on.' Me, Serena, and Gramps are starving," Rosanna announced, her large blue eyes gleaming with authority.

"She and Consuelo made pizza and lasagna. I helped. For dessert, we're having those ice cream balls I love," Serena said with reverence.

"They're called *tartuffo*. Dinner tonight consists of everything the girls love." Maria stood arched in the doorway.

Maria wore a frilly, white apron that said *Grandma Rules In The Kitchen*. Her silver hair, tied into a thick braid, hung down to her waist. Her cheeks were pink with heat. There were delicate lines at her mouth and eyes that came with age—she was, after all, an octogenarian. Maria was petite, but her indomitable character and personality were titanic.

"Have you completed your business?" Maria aimed dusky eyes at Isabella.

Isabella nodded. "We have, Mama."

"Everyone happy?" Maria looked around the room, knowing what was discussed.

Although Isabella ran her business on her terms, she often asked her mother for advice. Maria knew that Isabella had already decided to pass her company on to the next generation. What Isabella needed was reinforcement, and she got it. Maria wholeheartedly approved and encouraged Isabella's decision to move on and devote time to herself and her husband.

As much as Isabella loved her job and the company she built from the tailor shop her father left nearly bankrupt, four decades of fourteen-hour-seven-day workweeks took its toll physically and mentally on a person. The stress alone was enough to kill most, and Maria approved of Isabella stepping back to enjoy a life of leisure.

"We are thrilled, Gran." Bianca's lips ripe with the smile she hadn't been able to wipe off her face, she pecked Maria. "I'm going to be the CEO."

"Congratulations. You'll do a fine job, honey." Maria turned to Christian and pinched his cheek." So when can I expect those beautiful great-grandchildren?"

"Not you too, Gran."

"I'm not a spring chicken. I have limited time left, and I'd like to meet them before God takes me," Maria said.

"You are a spring chicken to me, Gran. A gorgeous one at that." Christian pecked Maria on the cheek and chained his arm through hers. "Come on, everyone. Gran wants us at the dinner table and gets what she wants. So move it."

Antonio's bemused eyebrow raised. The boy had derailed the conversation of great-grandchildren. A smooth operator was his son.

"We have to wait on Kat and Carlo," Isabella said.

"They've just pulled into the driveway with Gail and Marco and their brood," Maria said. "The family's all here. So, as Christian said, get your butts to the table. Antonio, honey, fetch a few bottles of wine from the wine cellar. Tonight, we celebrate the baton transfer from the current generation to the next, to Farfalla's future."

Chapter 2

CHRISTIAN OPENED THE DOOR TO Bianca's corner office and walked in. The room was brightly lit, with sunlight from the striking sun shining in a clear, blue sky. Out the corner glass walls, tall high-rise apartment buildings that had been built in the past twenty-five years to revive the downtown Toronto waterfront filled the landscape.

Isabella acquired the red-brick ten-story building on a dime from the former employer she drove into bankruptcy and worked with developers to transform the depressed commercial zone into a sprawling green urban space. Isabella surpassed her expectations. There were now walking and biking trails that blended with green spaces. The area boasted upscale bars, cafes and restaurants with outdoor patios. An IMAX theatre, a bike shop, and supermarkets that sold organic-only produce catered to the young professionals with disposable income who now populated the area.

It was urban renewal where young professionals wanted to live and be seen.

Bianca looked up from the financial statements in her hands at her brother. He wore black pants and a maroon silk shirt open at the neck. His thick curls had the windswept look he was known for, and his fashionable stubble was neatly trimmed.

"You could knock," Bianca said, sighing. She wore a tapered black jacket with thin lapels against a cream-coloured silk shirt and slim ankle pants. Her hair was bound into a smooth ponytail, and a black bow held it at the nape of her neck.

"Why? I didn't knock when Mom occupied this office, and she's more worthy of a knock than you," Christian said, walking to Bianca's desk.

Christian smelled the sweet scent of Amore that painted the air. Amore was Isabella's first venture into the perfume market and became her bestselling, and it was Bianca's favourite. Bianca didn't go a day without dabbing it on.

Bianca had changed little in the large corner office with a panoramic view of Lake Ontario and everything that had filled it for the past four decades. The art that hung on the steel-gray painted walls were framed pencil sketches of Isabella's first ten designs, which launched her career. The wood floor was the trademark chocolate-brown found at the Farfalla stores worldwide.

The desk was concave, with a high-gloss ebony top and sides and white leather sides. The executive chair, guest chairs, sofa, and matching chairs in the sitting area were plush, white Italian leather with polished nickel armrests. The coffee table was glossed walnut, as was the floating credenza against the wall.

Contemporary elegance was Isabella's style, and Bianca keenly embraced it.

"How's the making of your mini-mes coming along?" Bianca crossed to the credenza and picked up the pot of coffee resting on the hot plate. "All I ask is that none of the prospective concubine or incubator, whatever you want to call her, be from the office. I have too much to deal with right now to take on the aftermath of your jilted office romance."

Christian fell back into the soft leather of the guest chair. "Don't joke about that."

"I'm not. No fraternizing with the employees." Bianca's voice was firm.

"Message received." Christian nodded when Bianca waved a mug at him. "Can you see me settling down with one woman?"

"No, I can't, but it will happen. You just haven't met the right woman yet."

"I've met hundreds, maybe thousands…."

"Easy there, tiger."

"Well, I have met a lot of women and haven't met *her*. You really think she's still out there, and how will I know when I meet her?"

Bianca poured coffee into two white mugs with the word Farfalla in gold neon script printed across them. "For your sake, I hope you do. Mom's not letting up until she sees you married and giving her grandchildren."

"Yeah, don't I know it." Christian exhaled a long breath. "How will I know if and when I meet her?"

"You'll know." Bianca thought of the knock-out punch to the stomach she felt when she first saw Lorenzo. "The realization she's the one will come at you like a hand grenade to your system," Bianca added cream and sweetener to the coffee and wandered back to Christian. "Here, drink fast. I have more pressing matters to deal with than your love life. I need to prepare for my meeting with the bankers this afternoon to extend our loan and request another two hundred and fifty million dollars to finance the Asia expansion. No pressure."

"You're ready for it. I gave you the numbers I worked out and the paperwork you must present to the bankers." Christian sipped on the steaming coffee.

Bianca slid into the chair behind the desk. "You forget I inherited Mom's handicap for numbers, and all that finance gobbledygook makes me crazy. Add the pressure of proving myself a worthy replacement for Mom to those tight-ass bankers to get the financing we need."

"You got this. You have a business management degree from the best school, among the many other degrees. Put them to work."

Contemplatively, Bianca sipped at her coffee. "Mom had none of that higher education, and look what she accomplished. You're either born with the entrepreneurial gene or not."

"And you're the product of two of the best entrepreneur minds I know," Christian assured Bianca. "Cut yourself some slack. Besides, Dad will be in the meeting with you."

Bianca blew out a breath. "He cancelled a few minutes ago, citing some ridiculous excuse, which I translated to mean he wants me to go at this alone to prove I can do it."

"That is Dad's MO." Seeing the unease in his sister's eyes, Christian said, "Do you want me to come with?"

"Would you, Christian? I've memorized your data and financial statements. I think I can do this, but I'd feel more confident with you there."

"All you needed to do was ask."

Bianca's stomach stopped rolling, and the knots in her stomach loosened. Knowing she could still rely on her baby brother as she had since they were children was a comfort. "Thank you, Christian."

"You'll have to learn to ask for help, Bianca. Knowing your limitations is a sign of being a good leader. No one is impervious to limitations, and knowing when to ask for help makes or breaks you," Christian told her.

Bianca held her coffee cup in both hands and stared at Christian over the rim. "Since when did you become so wise?"

"I've always been wise. You just haven't noticed."

Bianca made a little snorting laugh. "The meeting is at three in the boardroom. I'll have my assistant, Joshua, email you the names of the attendees. It's a roster of the usual banking suspects."

"I'll look for the email and be there with my giant brain."

The snorted laugh was louder this time. "I never asked you how you feel about Mom giving me control of the company. Do you mind that she did?" Bianca asked after a short silence.

Blue eyes on blue eyes, Christian shook his head. "Why would I? You do all the work, and I still get half of this company."

She smiled at her brother's sensible response. "Well, yeah, there is that."

"I told you I have a big brain. Besides, I'm a numbers geek who is more suited to work in the background. I'm too pretty to be getting the stress wrinkles on this face your position brings on."

Bianca's mouth lifted at one corner. "I wish I was as confident as you. I'm starting to doubt myself, as everyone around here is. I don't know if I'm as capable as Mom of leading this company."

Christian waved a hand in dismissal. "Ignore the skeptics. It's easy to sit on the sideline and critique."

"Yeah, maybe." Bianca set her cup on the desk. "I've wanted this for so long. I studied for this, prepared for it, and now that I'm here, I'm doubting myself. The staff doesn't think I can do it. I see it in their eyes, hear it in their murmurs."

Christian studied his sister's defeated face. Bianca, the woman who was as tough as nails, allowing personal feelings and gossip to play havoc in her head, was a first. It was a vulnerable side of her rarely seen, and Christian needed to quash it if Bianca was to succeed at her first undertaking. Failure to secure the loan wasn't an option. It would psychologically impact her state of mind, and shaking it wouldn't be easy.

"Since when do you let what people think to colour your judgement? You, the woman whose motto is 'fuck 'em all.' All you need to know is that Mom and Dad have the confidence in you to do this, and they're rarely wrong. I can assure you that those who doubt you do because they know they cannot sit behind that desk and lead." Christian set the coffee mug on her desk and pushed to his feet. "I have the confidence in you that Mom and Dad do."

Bianca shrugged, but her poised gesture told him his words had restored her confidence. "Thanks, Christian."

"Anytime. I need to ensure my investment in the company remains profitable." Christian flashed her a full-on smile as he started to walk out of the office.

"Hey. What did you come in here for anyway?"

Christian stopped at the door. "Oh, yeah. I almost forgot. There's a reporter, Antonia Trenti, or maybe it was Trevi. Madeleine's message wasn't clear. She said the woman had a heavy Italian accent. This Antonia claims to be a reporter with Fashionista magazine, and she wants a meeting."

Bianca shook her head. "I've never heard of it or her. She may be a so-called influencer trying to get attention.

Have Madelaine pass the info on to marketing. Let them vet and deal with her."

"Okay," he glanced at his watch. I have to get back to the grind." Christian opened Bianca's office door and walked through it.

"Don't forget, three in the boardroom," Bianca called after him and returned to reviewing the paperwork for her first major meeting.

Getting the financing from the Bank of Commerce was tantamount to ensuring the company's expansion and the livelihood of the employees who depended on it. Feeling the pressure clamp down on her shoulders like a vice, Bianca forced her brain to shut down the worry and focused on the paperwork in her hands.

Chapter 3

THE TENSION IN the boardroom was as thick as the oak table they sat around. The blinds drawn closed for privacy, poised for battle, they sat on opposite sides—bankers versus business. In a sleek, tailored suit that exuded confidence, Bianca faced the three bankers, their expressions a mixture of skepticism and veiled condescension. The air crackled with unspoken judgment, the weight of expectations heavy on Bianca's shoulders.

The men were a carbon copy of each other. They wore navy suits, pressed white shirts, and red ties with the Bank of Commerce logo knit in gold. All three men displayed white pocket squares in their left breast pocket. Mr. Sorrel, Mr. Thomas, and Mr. Stuart—formality was a must for the old, stuffy men—sipped on coffee served in white China cups by Bianca's assistant. Bianca and Christian sipped on water from the bottle.

Framed photographs of models in various poses wearing Isabella Farfalla designs hung from the walls painted gold. At the center of the oval table, neatly displayed on a silver platter, were enough donuts, croissants, and bagels with an assortment of butter, strawberry jam, and cream cheese cups to feed an army. Eons ago, someone, somewhere, deemed noshing at boardroom meetings was an enticing prerequisite to a positive outcome. In Bianca's eyes, it wasted money, time, and effort.

Bianca stared at the three men, studying the financial packet she handed them on the proposed Asian expansion. She had meticulously prepared for the meeting, studying the financial forecasts and memorizing every detail of the

Asian expansion plan. Yet, as she began her presentation, the subtle dismissal in the bankers' eyes, their dismissive glances and patronizing remarks ignited a fire within her.

"As you can see, gentlemen, the projected ROI for the Asian market is significant, with exponential growth expected within three years." Bianca's voice was steady, laced with a steely resolve. Bianca wore no jewelry except for her wedding band because flashing valuable stones when asking for money wasn't a good idea. "Twenty-five exclusive Farfalla boutiques will be opened in the downtown core of major cities.

Mr. Sorrel, the eldest of the bankers, cleared his throat, his gaze lingering on Christian, who sat beside Bianca, his face an impassive mask. "China is a volatile market. Are you certain this is a wise investment, Christian?"

Before Christian could respond, she interjected, her voice firm and unwavering. "Mr. Sorrel, with all due respect, I am the CEO of this company, and I am confident in our strategy. We have assembled a team of experts with extensive experience in the Asian market, led by Tommy Lam, a specialist in Chinese startups."

"You're the numbers man, Christian. What do you say about the Farfalla Company risking one quarter billion dollars to break into unknown territory? One as unfamiliar as China," said Mr. Thomas.

Bianca's lips tightened into a thin line but let Christian respond when he squeezed her arm under the table.

"Bianca has the data on hand, Mr. Thomas. As the CEO, she can answer all of your questions." Christian pressed a hand to Bianca's knee under the table when her foot anxiously tapped on the tiled floor.

"We'd like to know what you think, Christian," said Mr. Stuart, never looking in Bianca's direction.

Bianca would be angry if she didn't pity them. Dismissing her as the men blatantly did portrayed them as closed-minded and intimidated by the presence of a powerful woman. She'd seen it too often with her mother during her tenure. Luckily for the world, like the dinosaurs, men like them were becoming an extinct breed.

Christian started to speak but closed his mouth when Bianca barrelled in with her response. "Mr. Sorrel, Mr. Thomas, and Mr. Stuart, I'm sure you received the memorandum advising I am now the company's CEO, taking over for my mother."

Mr. Thomas, with a penchant for condescension, leaned back in his chair, steepling his fingers. "While we appreciate your enthusiasm, Bianca, your experience is limited. You're requesting This significant loan, and we need assurance." Mr. Thomas's rotund face levelled on Bianca's as he twirled a ballpoint pen between his sausage-thick fingers.

Bianca met Mr. Thomas's gaze head-on, her blue eyes flashing fierceness rivalling her mother's. "I haven't been the face of the company until now. But Mr. Thomas, I've worked alongside my mother since I could walk. I know this company and its objectives far better than you give me credit for."

Mr. Stuart jumped to Mr. Thomas's defence. "We meant no disrespect, Bianca, but you must admit that your requisition of one-quarter of a billion dollars needs deep scrutiny." The owl-like eyes behind the thick lenses of his black, horn-rimmed glasses stared at Bianca.

"As a businesswoman, I can appreciate your circumspection. I certainly wouldn't hand over one dollar without due diligence." Bianca's face was serious.

"So, you can appreciate our position, can't you, Christian?" said Mr. Stuart.

Bianca stood, slapped her open hands on the table, and leaned forward. The piercing, narrowed eyes she aimed at the men had the fierceness of a pitbull poised to attack.

They would regret this, Christian thought, sitting back in his chair to enjoy the forthcoming show. When Bianca got her mad on, she could freeze hell over with a stare.

"Address me, gentlemen. I'm in charge of this company." Bianca leaned in a bit closer. "I appreciate your concern, Mr. Stuart, as much as you should appreciate my dismay at dismissing me on the premise of inexperience. Although I suspect it has more to do with me not having a tiny, shrivelling penis between my legs."

Bianca's satisfaction was immense at the instant and complete shock her comment provoked in the men.

Christian stifled the amusement on his face.

"Mrs. Romano, there's no need for such crudeness," huffed Mr. Thomas.

"I concur with Mr. Thomas," said Mr. Stuart.

Bianca swept her gaze over Mr. Sorrel. "We haven't heard from you. Do you have any thoughts?"

Gauging Bianca's fiery mood, Mr. Sorrel opted for a shake of his head.

"All right then. If this decision is difficult for you, gentlemen, I don't want to tax your limited intellect further. I'll place a call to Michael Lehman. You know your CEO. He and I went to school together. I'll put the burden on him to determine whether our two-billion-dollar company is worthy of the investment by the Imperial Bank. Thank you for coming, and I apologize for taking your time."

Mr. Sorrel shot to his feet when Bianca turned to head out of the conference room. "Mrs. Romano, Bianca, let's not be hasty and bother Mr. Lehman. He's a busy man. My colleagues and I can work this out … to your benefit."

Bianca paused with her hand on the doorknob. "How's that, Mr. Sorrel?"

"While you've been speaking, I've been reviewing Chris…." Mr. Sorrel paused when Christian subtly rolled his eyes and shook his head. "Your proposal and financial forecast, Bianca, and, um, I believe we can agree to authorize the loan."

Bianca swivelled to face Mr. Sorrell. "Only if you're sure, Mr. Sorrel. I wouldn't want to put you in a compromising position."

"I'm sure, Bianca. All we ask is that you agree to guarantee repayment of the entire loan amount if you are unsuccessful in your venture. Is that fair enough?" Mr. Sorrel looked at Mr. Thomas and Mr. Stuart, and both returned an assenting nod.

Bianca's ire rapidly evaporating, she nodded. "Fair enough, Mr. Sorrel. Send me the paperwork." Bianca stood at the doorway. "In the future, gentleman, picture your wife, daughter, mother, aunt, niece, or any important woman in your life in place of me and consider how they'd feel if, after all their hard work and accomplishments, they were shelved as insignificant because of their gender. How would you feel? No one, regardless of their gender, the colour of their skin, or station in life, should have to endure such degradation. Understood?"

The men nodded in unison and watched Bianca walk out of the boardroom.

Christian offered his hand, and the men shook it. "Between us guys, you only got a mild taste of the wrath of Bianca. Have a good day, gentlemen." Christian caught up with Bianca. "You didn't go to school with Michael Lehman,"

Bianca slid a glance over her shoulder. "They didn't know that."

Christian stared at her. "What if they turned you down?"

Bianca stepped into the elevator. "They wouldn't sacrifice losing our account. If they did, I know several banks lining up to take us on." She gave Christian a wink seconds before the elevator doors closed.

Chapter 4

THE RHYTHMIC PULSE of Italian music throbbed through the air at Santo's Ristorante. The lunchtime crowd buzzed with conversations and the clatter of cutlery. Christian's gaze was drawn to the woman perched on the barstool who looked like a vision in a cream-coloured dress that hugged fine curves.

Christian's eyes peered over the edge of his glass at the woman with the feline smile staring his way. She wore a skin-tight cream-coloured turtleneck dress that clung to her curvy body. The knee-high boots with spiked heels rode high on long legs. Her frosted blonde hair fell around a striking alabaster face with luminous blue eyes under mascara-darkened lashes. She had fire-red painted lips and the eye of every man in the room. But it was Christian she watched with interest.

In an automatic gesture, Christian lifted his glass in a toasting motion. His smile was big, and his eyes fiercely blue as he stared at her.

"Magnificent woman sitting at the bar staring at me," he murmured, a playful grin spreading across his face.

"There are two of us here, Christian. Perhaps she finds my rugged charm more appealing." Lorenzo cut into his chicken Marsala.

Christian scoffed. "One, I'm the hot babe at this table. Two, someone married to my sister shouldn't be saying that." Christian waved the waiter down.

"I am married to the most beautiful woman in the world, but I am not dead or blind." Lorenzo wore a gray cashmere rib-knit sweater opened at the collar and jeans.

His dark hair hung long and loose around his Olive-skin face.

"Gino, the blonde sitting at the bar, do you know who she is?" Christian asked when the waiter appeared at the table. Gino wore the Santo's black vest, pants, and white shirt uniform. A tea towel slung across one shoulder.

"Ah, the mystery blonde. Haven't seen her before." Gino picked up the empty beer bottle and glass off the table. "She's been turning heads all week."

Christian eyebrows winged. "You didn't even look at her."

"I know whom you speak of, Mr. Sabatini. You're not the first to ask." Gino reached for the tea towel on his shoulder and wiped the sweat rings the bottle left on the table.

"She does seem skilled in the art of flirtation." Lorenzo sopped Marsala sauce off the plate with a piece of bread.

"Would you like me to refresh her drink and bring you two beers and two espressos?" Gino hung the tea towel over his shoulder.

"It's like you read my mind. You know me so well. You do that, Gino." Christian watched Gino scurry toward the bar.

"He does know you well. He has known you since you were a horncat teenager." Lorenzo reached for another piece of ciabatta bread and sopped the remaining sauce on his plate.

"It's a horndog," Christian corrected.

Lorenzo's brow raised evenly. "Thank you for the correction, Mr. Horndog." Lorenzo stretched the word out in a sing-song manner. After a moment's study of the woman, Lorenzo said, "She is stunning, but something tells me that woman is fire and wind put into one, Christian."

"This comes from firsthand knowledge from being married to my sister. If so, add Satan into the mix. Don't tell Bianca I said that."

"No. It is intuition."

Christian smiled, reached for the bottle of beer Gino set on the table, and took a long pull. "Well, it would be fun to find out how hot she blows?"

"My guess is she heats to the melting point of gold, and you may be getting into something you cannot handle. Your women are—what do you call it?—arm candy." Lorenzo sipped on his beer. "That woman is not the arm candy type."

"We'll find out soon enough." Christian watched her slide off the barstool with one seamless move and saunter toward him. She brought with her the floral scent of *Amore* and drew the eye of every man in the room.

"I want to thank you for the drink." She was a head shorter than Christian's six-foot frame. Her teeth were very white and even. She wore a heart-shaped gold locket at her neck, and gold columns danced at her ears. She smelled heavenly. Picking up the salmon-coloured napkin off his lap, Christian rose, and her eyes followed him with an impressive gaze. "You are a tall one."

"I am, and you're very welcome. Please join us." Christian scraped the chair back before she could turn him down.

Flashing a sweet smile Lorenzo thought Toni put on for Christian's benefit, she sat. "I'd love to. Thank you."

"I'm Christian Sabatini, and this is my brother-in-law Lorenzo Romano."

"A pleasure. My name is Antonia Trevi." She held a perfectly manicured hand for Christian's, and his eyes zoomed in on her ringless finger. "My friends call me Toni with an I." She sat and crossed one slender leg over another. There was a lot of leg to cross, Christian thought.

"I hear a northern Italian accent, Toni." Lorenzo pushed his plate away and set his beer bottle in its place.

"I am from the Veneto region, but I spend much time travelling for my job." Her voice was like a melody, a captivating blend of Italian accent and sultry confidence.

Christian's lips twitched. "Well, Toni, with an I, can I get you another martini? Absolut with two olives, right?"

Toni's firm and full lips curved. Christian had been paying attention. "Thank you, but I think I have had enough." Toni picked up the biscotto that came with Christian's espresso, slid it between her lips, and bit into it. "You don't mind, do you?"

Christian shook his head. "What is it you do, Toni?"

Toni leaned in and folded her arms on the table. She rested her large breasts on her arms and was pleased to see Christian roll his eyes over them. "I write for Fashionista."

"You're the reporter who's been leaving messages asking for a meeting."

Toni's dimples flashed with charm. "I am. You are a difficult man to get a hold of," she said with a sexy Italian cadence that enchanted Christian.

Lorenzo cut Christian off when he started to speak. "Fashionista is a blog with five hundred followers. I have been to your site."

Toni bit back her irritation and pasted a soft smile on her face. "That's right. I never claimed to be a reporter. I said I was a writer, and it's a growing business." She turned away from Lorenzo's probing eyes to Christian. "I know it is nothing like what you have accomplished, but it is mine, and I enjoy it." Toni placed the remaining piece of biscotto between her teeth.

The woman made him dizzy. "What counts is that you enjoy your work."

Toni sucked the biscotto into her mouth. "A man who understands."

"I am the understanding sort."

With a mirroring smile, Toni said, "I just figured if I got an interview with you, my blog would…." Toni's face clouded, and she turned to Lorenzo for assistance in the translation. "*Come si dice esplodere*?"

"Blow up," Lorenzo offered, although he speculated her naïveté was an act.

"*Si*, blow up." Toni's eyes cut away from Lorenzo to Christian. "You have what it takes to provoke the attention of my readers."

"All five hundred of them," Lorenzo said under his breath, not buying Toni's act.

Focused on Toni, Christian missed Lorenzo's eye roll. "How about we discuss it further over dinner?"

Toni cocked her head and curved her lips into a broader smile. "I wish I could, but I have a previous engagement tonight. I will check my calendar and call you."

"Will you?" Christian said, watching Toni rise from the table.

Toni heard the desperation in Christian's voice and smiled. "Maybe I will, or maybe I won't." She sashayed away, leaving a lustful Christian pining for her.

"That woman is the essence of fire, wind, and Satan rolled into one," Lorenzo murmured.

Chapter 5

LORENZO STEPPED ASIDE to let Bob Klein, Tommy Lam, and Zane leave Bianca's office. The office was bright with sunshine, and the scent of freshly brewing coffee painted the air.

Lorenzo poked his head in. "Do you have a minute, Madam CEO?"

From behind her desk, Bianca looked up from the documents in her hand. "Just finished signing the bank documents for Mr. Sorrel."

Bianca's long hair was pulled back, setting off the dazzling blue eyes he loved to wake up to. She wore a mint-green sleeveless dress with a boat neckline. Pearls, the ones Lorenzo gave her on her last birthday, hung from her neck.

"I would not dismiss signing for a quarter billion dollar loan that simply. It is your first big accomplishment as CEO. Congratulations, *amore*." Lorenzo walked around the desk and leaned in to glide his lips over hers.

"The signing is not the accomplishment. It's that I made my voice heard at a meeting with three close-minded men and came out on top."

"'I am woman. Hear me roar.'" Lorenzo walked to the coffee machine and picked up the pot as the last drops of brewed coffee dripped.

"Exactly, and for you, my sexy husband, I have five minutes." Bianca placed the signed bank papers in the folder on the OUT tray before she rose from her chair behind the desk. "I have a ton of things to get to today."

"Before you join me on the sofa, call Joshua and ask him to bring you a sandwich and a salad." Lorenzo poured coffee into two cups.

Bianca shook her head. "I only have time for coffee."

Lorenzo returned the coffee pot to the hot plate and turned dark, persuasive eyes to look at Bianca, and she picked up the telephone to buzz Joshua.

Joshua was in her office before she returned the handset to its cradle. "What can I do for you, Bianca?"

Bianca picked up the folder from the OUT tray and handed it to Joshua. "Please make a copy of these documents for Christian, then run the originals to legal, Joshua," Bianca added when Lorenzo's eyes on her intensified. "And could you get me a garden salad and a ham and cheese sandwich on toasted white bread?"

"Sure thing, Bianca. Can I get you anything, Lorenzo?" Joshua gazed at Lorenzo with puppy-love eyes.

"No, thank you, Joshua, but I would like you to call me if you see my wife not eating the food she ordered. As her assistant who knows her every move, I am putting you in charge of reporting her eating habits to me." Lorenzo strolled to the sitting area and handed his wife the cup of coffee.

Bianca saw the flush of panic come over Joshua's face, and she made a sound between a sigh and a grumble. "Ignore my husband, Joshua. That's his attempt at humour."

"It is, Joshua." Lorenzo sat next to his wife on the sofa.

The relief on Joshua's face was huge. "Oh. Okay."

"Thank you, Joshua. Please close the door behind you." Alone in the office, Bianca said, "Don't tease him like that. If you haven't noticed, he has a man crush on you."

Lorenzo's brow winged. "I did miss that, but I understand it. Who would not want all this handsomeness." Lorenzo's comment elicited a snort from Bianca.

"He's not gay."

Lorenzo swiped his forehead with two fingers. "That is good to know, especially since I am married to you. But do not change the topic. Coffee is not a food group, and I need someone to keep track of you to ensure you eat right."

"I spoke to Mom," Bianca said, aiming to change the topic again.

Lorenzo resigned himself to failure and joined in the conversation. "Isabella is checking up on you?" he said, taking a swig of the coffee.

Bianca cupped her coffee cup and sipped. "I called her. I wanted to check in on how their first post-retirement vacation was going, and it sounds as if it's going well. She and Dad will spend two weeks at Uncle Carlo's place in Lago di Garda before meeting with Kat and Uncle Carlo in Milan for fashion week. Do you believe Kat will be Uncle Carlo's lead model at fifty-nine?"

"I do. She is still as hot-looking as when your mother discovered her." Lorenzo caught Bianca's dramatic brow raise and added, "Never as hot as you, of course."

Bianca's mouth lifted at one corner. "Good save. But yes, you're right. She does look pretty hot, still." Bianca conceded.

"Fifty-nine is the new forty, but I mean it when I say that you look as good as a high fashion model. And remember, I've seen you naked. Not in a while, but last I saw you naked…." Lorenzo exhaled a long breath.

Now she laughed. "All right. That's enough kissing up."

"Am I making you rethink the naked thing?" Lorenzo said with a wicked wiggle of his eyebrows. "Joke aside, who better than Kat, the woman who knows Carlo's designs best, to walk his collection down the runway at Milan Fashion Week?

"Agreed, and it is smart to use Kat's celebrity to launch the spring line before we venture into Asia," Bianca said, and Lorenzo nodded in agreement. "You know she has fifty million followers on Instagram and as many on TikTok."

"I do know this. I am a follower." The comment got Lorenzo a surprised look. "Yes, I am on TikTok. Serena set up an account for me. Did you tell your mother about getting the loan?" Lorenzo jumped in to say when Bianca started to laugh.

"I did. She'll pass the message to Carlo that we're good to go on the launch of our first Farfalla-Mesi venture," Bianca said with quiet pleasure.

Lorenzo drank the rest of the coffee and set the empty cup down on the edge of the coffee table. "Farfalla & Mesi will be the Dolce & Gabbana of Asia. When will you announce the two companies are working together? This will be very big. The Isabella Farfalla Fashion Company, joining forces with her brother's multi-billion dollar company, will rock the fashion world. You will become the most prominent fashion house in the world."

Lorenzo's eyes twinkled, and Bianca thought there was nothing sexier.

"We plan to announce it mid-year, six months before the first boutique opens. We're still working the kinks out of the marketing campaign. That's why Zane, Tommy Lam, and Bob met with me. Bob says his Chinese contact assured him documents and construction are on schedule. Zane asked for more people to help him with the campaign."

"Makes sense. The marketing must be done correctly for a successful launch."

"Agreed. The campaign covers all media: social, newspapers, magazines, television, and radio. We're also working on an Asian fashion week extravaganza. Our focus right now, though, is the website and social media. I told Zane to hire as many people as he needs." Bianca kicked her shoes off, tucked her legs under her and leaned back. "I saw your summer designs."

"You liked them." He watched her sink deep into the soft leather cushions. She looked comfortable and relaxed, a sight he had rarely seen lately.

"The entire collection is stunning, Lorenzo. Mom is right. You do have a special talent." Bianca called out at the knock on the door, "Come in."

Joshua took several steps into the room. When Bianca waved him in, Joshua proceeded to the sitting area and set the lunch tray on the coffee table. "I got you a sandwich and a salad, too, Lorenzo. You can join Bianca and make sure she has her lunch." The words tapered off to a faint smile, then a broader one when Lorenzo threw back his head and laughed.

"Well played, Joshua."

"Thank you. I'll leave you to it." Joshua started for the door, stopped, and turned.

Bianca and Lorenzo looked at Joshua. When he remained watching them, Bianca nudged him along. "What is it, Joshua?"

"I wanted to…." Joshua stopped when nerves got to him.

Bianca could hear Joshua breathing fast, and she said, "Take a deep breath, Joshua. What's our company motto?"

"'Say what's on your mind,'" Joshua recited, taking a deep breath for courage. "I wanted to ask Lorenzo if I could work with him. Not that I don't like being your assistant, Bianca, but I want to become a designer, and I'd really, really, really like to work with Lorenzo. I took the assistant position because it was the only one available, and although I'm qualified for it, designing is what I really want to do. I'm sorry." Joshua sucked in a deep breath.

"I see," Bianca said.

Joshua rambled on. "I figured, as your assistant, it would get me in the door and eventually to Lorenzo. He's the best designer I know, and I want to learn everything from him. Everything. I have a portfolio of my designs. I've wanted to be a designer since I started putting pencil to paper when I was five. I've wanted to be a designer since then. I would've loved working with Isabella, but she's no longer here. Not that I think you're second best, Lorenzo, because you're certainly not that and…. I'm just going to shut up now," Joshua said, feeling his face hot when he felt the weight of their stare on him and the stress of tears coming on.

"Well, that is certainly speaking your mind." Lorenzo watched Bianca bite down on her lower lip to keep herself from laughing. "What do you say, Bianca? Can you spare Joshua? I want to give him a chance to get a taste of designing with a second-rate mentor and see if that's what he truly wants to do with his life?"

Joshua dropped his gaze. "Oh, Jesus."

"Only if Joshua thinks he can handle dealing with your second-rate humour day in and day out. Can you handle it, Joshua?"

Joshua flicked his eyes from the ground to Bianca and then Lorenzo. "Yes. Yes, I can."

"It is set. Report to design on Monday, Joshua, and bring your portfolio. I want to take a look at it," Lorenzo said.

"Yes, sir, will do. I'll be there first thing Monday morning." Joshua left the office, and Bianca and Lorenzo thought they saw a bounce in his step.

"Now…."

Lorenzo cut Bianca off. "Eat and talk and tell me about our new venture with the Mesi fashion house."

Bianca poured olive oil and a spritz of lemon onto her salad and tossed it. She forked the salad, brought it to her mouth, and read Lorenzo in on the plan.

Half an hour later, with the ragged edges of the day smoothed away, Bianca said, "What do you say to see me naked tonight?"

Lorenzo stopped his sandwich mid-way to his mouth. "Do not toy with my hormones."

"I thought maybe we could check into a room at the Royal York Hotel for the night after work."

The sparkle in Lorenzo's eyes gave her his answer. "I will call Nanny to let her know to watch over the girls." His enthusiasm made Bianca laugh.

Chapter 6

THE VAULTED CEILINGS of Santo's Ristorante absorbed the sound of people talking, clinking glasses, and cutlery clanking on China, pouring wine, and the music flowing from speakers. The scent of expensive perfume and good food hung in the air.

Christian felt Toni's aura the minute she walked in. Only hers. He thought a hush fell when she appeared to float across the room, her hips seductively swaying. Her ripe breasts spilled over the square neckline of the tight-fitting black ribbed knit dress that emphasized everything with great detail. Diamonds glinted at her ears, neck, and wrist. Her blonde hair haloed her face, and her lips were painted her trademark fire-red—and fire she was.

Lorenzo's warning rang in Christian's head, but he wouldn't mind flying close to that flame.

The maître d', a twenty-something perky brunette, escorted Toni to Christian's table, where he anxiously waited. Every man in the restaurant cast eyes on her, and every woman resented her. She was the kind of woman that men—and women, for that matter—looked at twice.

"You're half an hour late." Christian sat when she sat.

Toni's lips slowly curved. "It is called being fashionably late. I can leave if you are disappointed."

Christian shook his head emphatically. "I don't want you to leave. I'm sorry for the outburst, but I'm not used to being made to wait by anybody."

"I am not anybody."

"No. No, you're not that."

"I am sorry. Forgive me."

Blue eyes steady on blue eyes, he held her gaze intently. She was too deep in him for him to be angered by her fruitless apology. "Because I am the forgiving type, I will. This time."

Toni tossed her hair, sending waves of platinum blonde in the air and cascading around her face down to her shoulders. "And am I not worth the wait?"

Christian eyed her from head to toe. "You are indeed. The three weeks I waited for you to call were well worth it." Christian wore a sky-blue silk shirt that traced sinewy arms and navy pants with knife-edged pleats. "

Toni gave Christian a flirtatious sideways look. "It is crass for a girl to be too obvious. Besides, I have been busy."

The woman intrigued him. "I hope you don't mind. I ordered for you," Christian said when Gino set the martini on a coaster before her.

Toni shook her head. "A martini hits the spot." Toni slowly sipped her drink and imprinted red lipstick on the rim of the glass.

"How have you been keeping busy?" Christian asked more out of a need to know who she was spending her time with than out of curiosity.

Toni leaned back in her chair and crossed her legs, making the dress ride up to expose more of her creamy-white thigh. Her thigh looked solid and smooth. Christian approved. "I could say you are too nosy or possibly jealous."

"Possibly a little of both." Christian saw the candle's flame flicker in her mischievous eyes.

"Good." Toni went silent when Gino appeared with the Caesar salads and a bottle of Giuseppe Quintarelli, which Christian sampled. On Christian's approval, Gino poured red wine into two glasses and left. "You do take— how do you say?—liberties."

"I had half an hour to kill, so I ordered our drinks and meal. I thought you'd like the wine. It's from the Veneto region. If you don't, Gino can take it back and cancel the meal." Christian sipped on his wine.

Toni heard the irritation in his voice, and her lips curved. "Not necessary, but do not do it again. I do not like a man who takes charge of me."

Christ! The woman drove him crazy. "I won't. Does that mean we'll be doing this again?"

Toni speared salad with her fork. "I will let you know at the end of the night," she said.

Her sultry voice conjured thoughts in his head. Pleasurable thoughts. The rush of forbidden anticipation was immediate.

Gino appeared at their table several more times to refresh empty glasses and replace empty dishes with cheese tortellini. They followed that with Osso Bucco with mushrooms in a wine sauce and panna cotta for dessert.

Christian spoke mainly about himself during the meal, but Toni didn't mind. She wanted to know everything there was to know about Cristian Sabatini, and his male ego was happy to oblige.

"You are a very accomplished man, Christian. I admire a skillful man." Toni watched the flush of pleasure rise to his cheeks.

"I'm a skillful man in many areas." Christian's reply caused Toni to lift a brow.

"Not in the department of humility."

His eyes crinkled. She got his juices flowing. His desire to taste those kissable lips was the strongest he had ever felt for any woman.

"By the way, you look great and smell amazing." Christian reached for his espresso.

"It is your scent, *Amore*, and what I am wearing is one of Lorenzo's designs. The man is very talented."

Jealousy flared in Christian's eyes. "He's also very married to my sister."

Toni tsked at him. "There is that green-eyed monster again."

It was past eleven, and the restaurant was nearly empty and quieter. Over the speakers, Dean Martin's baritone voice joyfully proclaimed it was *amore*.

"Me, jealous of that Italian gigolo." Christian's jealousy filled his voice.

"Yes, you are, but you do not have to be." Toni leaned in and touched her lips with his. "How about we get out of here and head to your place for a nightcap," she whispered in his ear.

A huge smile spread across his face. Christian's head was swimming with anticipation, and his hand shot up to signal Gino for the check.

Chapter 7

THEY DIDN'T BOTHER with the nightcap. Toni and Christian headed straight for his bedroom, leaving a trail of discarded clothes.

Christian's bedroom was a manly oasis of charcoal-gray, black, and rich brown woods. The focal point, a king-size floating bed covered in white Egyptian cotton and down pillows of different sizes, stood at the centre of the large room. Beneath it, the thick charcoal-coloured carpet rode high to the ankles.

Above the dark oak dresser hung an enormous flat-screen television. Framed oils of Formula One racing cars and sailing boats covered the remaining charcoal-painted walls. Two potted palm trees at opposite ends of the glass wall opened to a balcony with a view of the gardens and pool, now blanketed in snow. The only light in the room was from the blue LED glowing beneath the bed, but it was enough for him to see Toni in all her naked splendour.

Al Green's "Let's Stay Together" softly floated from the speakers.

Toni's skin was golden-brown and silk-smooth. Her curves were sensual. Her breasts were large, two perfect spheres with dark nipples. Although Christian was sure silicone had a hand in their flawlessness, they were too spectacular to care either way.

"You're impressive and stunning." He pulled her into his arms and held her tight. Her body was warm against his, and the spear of lust arrowed straight to his loins.

"Ditto." Toni traced small circles on the steel-hard chest and ran her fingers up his arms and across the broad shoulders. Toni circled his naked body and took him all in. He was exquisite, with solid shoulders, a tapered waist, a tight butt, and powerful legs. "Yes indeed, you are impressive and stunning," she said approvingly.

"I try." Christian picked her up and carried her to the bed.

Looking up into the eager blue eyes, she said, "I don't sleep with just any man, especially not on a first date."

"I should hope not." Christian buried his face in her neck and feathered it with slow, sumptuous kisses.

"I also don't like to be taken advantage of."

"It's not my style." He slithered his tongue down the valley between her breasts.

"What is your style?"

Christian's gaze fastened on her eyes. "Pleasing a woman and fulfilling her every need as she deserves. Would you like that?"

"I would." Toni hadn't finished saying the words when he clamped his mouth on her breast and bit down on her nipple.

Moaning, she arched and drove her breast deeper into his mouth. Suckling on them, he ignited the fire she wanted through her. Her heart pounded faster in her chest, and her breaths came ragged.

His objective to get to know her had his mouth moving down to her flat stomach and thighs. Her dazed look came with shocking delight when he spread her legs and slithered his fingers to explore and please as he promised. She was close to orgasm when his tongue took her to taste heat and woman.

Her body suffused with a wonderful pleasure before the shockwave from the orgasm he drove in her sent her shuddering and crying out his name and begging for more.

Christian made her blood heat and swim. Her breath trembled in, then out. Her eyes rolled back as he took her up and over again. When she thought he was through with her, she felt the jolt of the intense third orgasm shoot through her body.

He moved above her, and his clean, manly scent slid into her. "Have I pleased you?" he said, gazing into her contented eyes.

Breathless, she smiled up at him. "*Gesù Cristo, si.*" Her voice was subdued and sleepy.

Brushing his lips to hers, he said, "Given that means yes tenfold, will you please me now?"

She nodded and opened up to him. Taking her mouth, he kissed her as he pierced her and buried himself inside her. His connection with her brought an inexplicable and extraordinary shock to his system. She stirred something in him no other woman had. In one fast, unrelenting wave, she resurrected feelings he hadn't felt before.

Arching against him, she wrapped her legs around his waist. "You are not thinking of stopping now," she said when he momentarily froze.

Shaking his head, he covered her mouth with his. His mouth on hers was full of energy, and the feeling of need in the kiss was potent and obvious.

Christian thought he heard the choir of angels as he moved in and out of her slowly, lovingly. He made the moment and feelings engulfing him last as long as possible. He wished it could go on forever, but his body tightened. His blood roared in his head, and his breath quickened as his final hard drive into her filled her.

Christian rolled off Toni onto his side. She could see his chest gleaming with a light sheen of sweat in the dim light of the bedroom. He was sexy and beautiful.

Toni brushed her lips to his, sweetly, tenderly. "You were incredible." The kiss deepened to express her gratitude.

"I was good, wasn't I," he said with humour in his eyes.

"Are you sure you are an accountant? I have always heard they were geeks, and you are not that."

Throwing his head back, Christian let out a booming laugh. "I guess I'm one of the rare accountants that bypassed the geek gene." Christian lifted her hand and brought it to his lips. "But I think it's more that you make me good."

"I do?" Toni leaned into him. She caught sight of the small vertical scar above his right brow and ran a finger over it.

"Bianca pushed me off my bike when I was five, and my face scraped the pavement." Christian buried his face in her hair and breathed in the scent of lilac.

"That was not very nice."

"I'm her baby brother, and it's what older siblings do. Do you have any brothers or sisters?" Christian got out of bed, stumbled into his boxers, and walked to the dresser. Toni followed him with her eyes. His hair was unruly, his bare arms were muscled, and his bare chest was hard as steel. He was a remarkable sight.

Picking up the remote off the dresser, he pressed a button, and the panels slid open to expose a bar complete with a mini-fridge and shelves stocked with quality bottles of spirits, a fully stocked wine rack, and a selection of glasses.

"Cristal?" Christian asked. When she nodded, he reached into the refrigerator and retrieved the bottle.

"I wish I had a sister or a brother, but no, it is just me." Toni watched him expertly cut off the foil on the bottle, untwist the cage and pop the cork.

Christian brought two flutes of champagne to bed. He set the bottle on the night table. "I must admit, as much as Bianca and I butt heads, I like the idea of an older sister looking out for me." He slid into the bed next to her.

"It does sound nice, you know, to have someone look after you," Toni said, sipping on Cristal. The fizz of champagne on her tongue tingled.

Christian picked up a lock of her hair and twined it around his finger. "I can look after you."

"How do you not know I am not some kind of evil mastermind after your money?" Toni's eyes were on him intently as she drank.

"A woman who ties me up in knots as no woman has could never be an evil mastermind." Christian smiled at Toni.

Toni sat up in bed and stared at him. "What are you talking about tying you up in knots? We had dinner and jumped into bed, and suddenly, I am tying you up in knots."

Christian glided his lips over hers. "Not suddenly. You tied me in knots from the moment we met. For the three weeks after the day we met, you didn't call, and I was going crazy out of my mind. When you finally called and heard your voice, it felt like I'd scaled Mount Everest."

The weight of his words hung heavy in the air, and she saw the emotions in his eyes with perfect clarity. "*Gesù*! You do not know me, Christian."

"But I do. You're thirty-six, you have a journalism degree, you love to travel and cook…."

"You have been reading my blog." Toni jumped in to say.

"You better not be underage. I can end up in jail after what I did to you." There was humour in his voice.

She rolled her big blue eyes. "I am thirty-six but do not know how to fry an egg. That is just stuff you put on a blog bio for readers."

"I'll get to know you. I want to get to know you, Antonia Trevi." He lowered his forehead to hers. "Will you stay the night? I want to wake up next to you in the morning. We can spend the weekend together."

Very little could have pleased Toni more than to hear those words, but she said nothing. Pushing off the bed, she wrapped her naked body in the bedsheet and walked to the window. They were silent for a while as she stood staring out the window with him watching her.

The moon had reached its apex in a black sky and shadowed the snow-covered land. In the distance, she saw two pairs of eyes glinting in the dark, scurrying raccoons, foxes, or possibly coyotes. A cold breeze moved through the air, making a soft, fluting sound against the glass. It felt soothing and calm, unlike what she felt inside.

Toni turned to face Christian, stretched out on the bed, propping himself on his elbow. "I'll stay, but only if you promise me one thing."

Christian watched her silhouetted in the silvery moonlight that streamed through the window. "Anything."

She took a deep breath and let it out. "You cannot fall in love with me, Christian. This is just a bit of fun between us."

She was in his head, his blood as no other woman had been before, and he couldn't seem to shake her. "I can't promise that."

"Promise me, Christian, or I will leave, never to see you again." She held her gaze on him and, in her eyes, saw she meant it.

"All right, I promise," he said because he didn't want her to leave.

If there was one thing Christian hadn't factored in, it was falling in love with her as hard as he was.

Chapter 8

SINKING BACK IN her chair, Bianca studied the man before her. He was five feet three inches tall, and Bianca concluded that what they said about men who lacked stature, making it up in obnoxiousness, was accurate.

The man was plump and wore a gray three-piece suit. His dark hair was liberally salted. His green eyes and mouth were etched with the lines and crevices that gave men a distinguished look, but none of that helped. No matter how he cleaned and dressed it up, Bob Klein was nothing more than a ginormous asshole.

On top of the everyday stresses of running a business at her young age, Bianca wondered how her mother had dealt with the blatant chauvinism she had to deal with from closed-minded men. More importantly, why would she have to? A couple of anatomical differences between the sexes were no reason for some men to feel superior to their female counterparts.

It was the twenty-first century for chrissakes. Assholdry, however, appeared to be a timeless art.

"I'm the best Vice President of International Sales you've had," Bob Klein said huffily.

Twirling the pen between her fingers and thumbs, Bianca gave Bob the stone-face stare she had mastered from watching her mother all those years she had been training to step into her shoes. "We've had five complaints, Bob, including one from your assistant who has filed an official sexual harassment complaint against you." Bianca wore a white pantsuit and a silk lavender blouse with a laced bow at her neck.

Bob leaned back in his chair and pressed his lips together. "Pfft, Margie. The woman is an uptight twenty-nine-year-old spinster. She interprets every man's gesture as a sexual attack on her person."

Bianca's brows met in a frown. Who said on her person? The man was stuck in a long-dead decade.

"She says," Bianca flipped the manila folder open and went through the stack of papers until she found Margie's signed complaint amongst the others. "And I quote, 'Bob Klein stood up behind his desk, and stroked his crotch with his index finger, slowly, deliberately, in a suggestive manner while I went over the agenda for the day.'"

Bob stifled a boyish giggle. "I had an itch. That's all it was. It was an itch that needed scratching," he stressed when Bianca's slim brows knit in doubt.

"That comment doesn't help your case, Bob. Did you also have a so-called itch when," Bianca continued to read the complaint. "'He walked up behind me and began to, unwarrantedly, massage my shoulders. Next thing I know, his hand is cupping my breast, squeezing it. I froze. I didn't know what to do. I felt so violated and dirty that I went home and showered for the rest of the night to wash his repulsiveness off me.' Why would you think an unsolicited sexual gesture from a septuagenarian man would be remotely attractive to a young woman?" Bianca fell silent to allow that to sink in.

Bob dismissed the comment with a wave of his hand. "I've generated millions of dollars in sales for your mother, for this company, Bianca. Hundreds of millions of dollars to date," he repeated to drive the point. "I've worked my ass off the entire time I've been here."

"Your work performance is not in question, Bob. It has been commendable. You could have worked for me for another twenty years." Bianca rose, rounded her desk and leaned a hip on it, her arms folded. "But, Bob, this is a female-owned company. How would it look if I championed what HR, after an extensive internal investigation on you, deemed as sexual predatory?"

After what Isabella endured at Joe Smith's hands, after the distress, fear, and anger she carried with her for years, Isabella vowed no one in her company would suffer such abuses from man or woman. Bianca promised to enforce the policy established by her mother not only because she was a staunch believer that no one, male or female, should endure bullying but also because her employees deserved a safe work environment.

"Christ, sexual predator. That's harsh when it's nothing but meaningless banter," Bob said.

"No, Bob, it's not just meaningless banter and the sexual predator label applies. We've had you under investigation for the past two years."

Bob's spine stiffened when it hit him. "Isabella initiated the investigation? After everything I did for her and the sales I generated for her company. Christ! It's me who brokered your entry into the Chinese market."

"She did, Bob. As much as she hated to do it, she asked for the investigation immediately after the first complaint against you was brought to HR. It's all in here." Bianca picked up the thick file on her desk and waved it at Bob. "Every sordid recording of your conversations, copies of unsolicited emails to several of our female interns, and photographs."

"You can't do that without my consent," Bob defiantly huffed.

"We can, Bob. It's a company-owned telephone, computer, car, and office. We can do what we want."

Bob's shoulders slumped. "It's all a misunderstanding. I didn't mean any of it, Bianca."

"It's not a misunderstanding, and you meant every word, Bob. It's been a consistent and systematic act of harassment on your part. I want you to clean out your office. As we speak, an email announcing your departure from the company is being sent."

Bob's foot tapped nervously on the floor. "I'm sixty years old. How am I supposed to find a job at this age?"

"You should have thought of that before you set off to harass our employees sexually, Bob." Bianca rounded her desk and sat in her chair again.

Anger took over, and Bob propelled to his feet, plunked hands, palms down on her desk. "I'll sue you and this goddamn company for every penny."

Bianca leaned forward, her eyes held firmly on Bob's. "It's your right, Bob, but remember that today is your last payday."

"You can't do that."

Bianca leaned back in her chair and crossed her legs. "And that bonus you were expecting is null and void."

"I worked my fingers to the bone for that bonus. I'm entitled to it." Bob's voice hitched one octave.

"Not according to your contract. My mother put a nifty clause in all the Farfalla employee contracts that states you forfeit all bonuses due to egregious behaviour. I'd consider sexual harassment egregious. And there's so much incriminating evidence we have on you." Bianca waved the file in the air before pressing the intercom button on her telephone to buzz Joshua's replacement.

"Leslie, have security come to my office to escort Mr. Klein out."

"Is that necessary?" Bob barked.

"It's company policy, Bob." Bianca's calm and deliberate voice was rankling him now.

"I'm the vice president of goddamn international sales."

Bianca's shoulders lifted and dropped. "Off the record, Bob, and to quell my curiosity, why do it? Let me rephrase the question. How would you feel if the man, your daughter, granddaughter, wife, or any woman you love were made to endure unwanted sexual advances that poisoned their work environment to the point that it became difficult for them to get out of bed and go off to a job they enjoyed?" Bianca waited a beat for a response, but none followed.

"How would you feel if they were made to feel vulnerable and powerless to do anything about it? How would you feel if their confidence and trust were stolen from them for no reason other than doing their job?" Again, Bianca waited for a response, but all Bob did was scrub his hands over his face. "Well, Bob, I hope they never have to endure such a traumatic experience that imbues a sense of shame and guilt that stays with you all your life." It stayed with her mother for decades.

When Leslie opened the door to Bianca's office, Bianca waved the security guards in. "Escort Mr. Klein to his office. Leslie, please ensure someone from HR meets them there to oversee Mr. Klein packing his things. Also, have them collect all company property from Mr. Klein before he leaves the building."

"You're going to regret this, Bianca. I'm going to make you regret it," Bob repeated as the security guards forcefully escorted him out of her office.

Chapter 9

CHRISTIAN WALKED INTO Bianca's office without knocking. The sun that had shone all day through the south-facing window of her office was replaced by a bright moon sliced in half-ringed with stars as clear as glass.

Bianca's usually orderly desk was covered in files. Bianca was so focused on the paperwork before her that she didn't see Christian standing before her desk. He stood before her for some time in that suspended way people do when waiting for someone to acknowledge them.

Christian cleared his throat.

"Jesus." Startled, Bianca looked up.

Christian wore jeans, a white shirt, sleeves rolled to the elbow, and black loafers. The stress of the long workday didn't show on his handsome face—it never did. Bianca hated him for that.

"How long have you been standing there?" Bianca set the pen on the desk and stretched the cramp out of her hand.

Christian held the bottle of Jameson Irish Whiskey in his hand. "Thought you could use a drink. I know I can."

Bianca glanced at her laptop for the time. "Six o'clock already. Where has the day gone?" She rose to stretch her legs. "Pour. A double."

"Long day?" Christian poured the whiskey into lowball glasses.

"They seem to get longer and longer." Bianca shrugged off the tailored jacket, kicked off her shoes, and stretched out on the sofa.

"Yeah, Dad lied to me when he told me year-ends got easier with experience." Cristian handed her one of the glasses in his hands.

Contemplatively, she drank. "Mom made it look so easy."

"Both of them did." Christian sat in the chair across from her. "You will, in time."

"You just said you haven't."

"I said year-ends. Most of the accounting year is easy to handle. It's a matter of getting into a routine, a rhythm. You know?"

"I don't know if that's possible." Bianca tipped back her head and closed her eyes.

"Sure it is. You're very much like mom."

"I don't know about that." Bianca took a long sip. The whiskey went down like liquid silk and loosened the knots on her shoulders and belly. "Christ, I needed that. So many fires come up daily that I'm now responsible for putting out. Today's leaned more toward the dumpster fire category."

"I heard about Bob." Christian stretched out and put his feet on the coffee table, crossing them at the ankles.

"That was a party." Bianca downed the last of her drink and held out the glass to Christian for a refill.

Cristian picked up the bottle and poured whiskey into her glass. "How did he react to you firing him?"

"He threatened to sue us." Bianca unlaced the bow at her neck and unbuttoned the top two buttons of her shirt.

"You think he'll go through with it?"

"I hope not. If Bob goes through with the lawsuit, it may not bode well for our Asian launch. Those uptight bankers may decide not to get caught up supporting a company with a high-profile sexual harassment case and call the loan."

"Then why did you antagonize Bob by getting security to escort him out and make him do the Cersei walk of shame to his office?"

"I couldn't let him walk out with his dignity intact. I had to give his inflated ego a grounding and hopefully give the women he harassed some form of closure. I know it's not much, but it's the best I can do for now. I'll work out something to counter his indefensible actions and give the women proper closure." Bianca's contemplative look told Christian her mind was already working on a plan.

"I know you will. I never imagined Bob to be a predator. Mom has such a good radar for this type of thing. I'm surprised she didn't catch it sooner."

"Well, she eventually did. It took her a few years, but she sensed something was up solely based on Margie's mannerisms around him. The moment her radar went off, she chatted with Margie and got her to spill her guts. Mom encouraged Margie to submit a complaint to HR and immediately launched an investigation."

Christian slapped his glass on the armchair, spilling whiskey over its lip. "Christ, the man is a husband, a father, a grandfather to impressionable young girls."

Bianca loosened her hair and let it fall around her face. "Imagine tonight's dinner conversation."

"I doubt he'll tell his wife. Not right away, anyway. No man would."

Bianca shot Christian a look from under her lashes. His day's worth of stubble was dark against his skin.

"She'll find out. I can't tell you more than that," she said, anticipating the oncoming question. "Not out of spite, but out of female solidarity."

"Mrs. Klein may refuse to admit her husband of forty years could be a sexual predator." Christian drank some of his whiskey.

"Forty years with the man tells me she's known what her husband is made of all along, and that denial is emblematic of her refusing to accept it."

"Either way, this puts a kink into the Asian launch of the Farfalla-Mesi boutiques."

"It does and becomes another fire I must put out. And I will, just not tonight. I need to sleep on it. I need a clearer head to focus on the issue." Bianca angled her head toward the door when Lorenzo peeked his head in. The bright smile he aimed at her lightened her ugly mood. He always seemed to bring the sunshine with him. "Come join us, honey. We're drinking our very long day away."

"Grab a glass," Christian pointed toward the credenza, "if you want to join us in our misery."

"I have had a good day, but I will join you anyway." Lorenzo wore pleated gabardine pants, gray, a black shirt with a matching tie, and a cream-coloured vest. Lorenzo took the seat beside Bianca. "You all right, *amore*? I heard about Bob."

Bianca nodded. "I'd rather not talk about Bob anymore. Every time I think about him, my blood boils."

Lorenzo looked over to Christian. "What is tying up your underwear?"

"I, brother-in-law, go commando most days. I don't wear underwear," Christian explained when Lorenzo's brow creased.

"Christ, there's an image I need acid washed from my brain," Bianca said, and both men laughed. "How women flock to you is a mystery for the ages. Tell us about your day, honey. You said it was a good one."

"It was. It turns out Joshua has a lot of potential. He is very talented, and his talent comes from here." Lorenzo pressed a hand to his heart. "You cannot teach that. Better than that, he is eager and thirsty for learning."

"Good, so you'll take him under your wing and teach him all?" Bianca wiggled her foot, and Lorenzo massaged the sole.

"Yes, I will be his mentor. He is eager to learn everything I have to teach. I will mould his mind and shape his artistic talent into our vision. I will make him as good as me." The excitement in Lorenzo's voice made Bianca's lips curve into a smile. "On our next trip to Milan, I thought we would take him and show him the Mesi operation. He would be thrilled to meet Carlo, the man behind the Mesi brand."

"Uncle Carlo will like that. You know how supportive he is of upcoming designers." Bianca watched her brother's eyes turn wistful as he sipped on his drink. "If I know my brother, that goofy look on his face tells me it involves a woman."

"It is goofier than usual. She must be special," Lorenzo said.

"Not that it's any of your business, but yes. I spent the weekend with Toni."

After a beat, Lorenzo said, "The woman we met at Santo's Ristorante a few weeks ago."

Bianca caught the look Christian and Lorenzo exchanged. "You didn't tell me about her, and it sounds like you should have."

"You don't need to worry about Lorenzo. She only has eyes for me." Christian reached for the whiskey bottle from the coffee table and refilled everyone's glasses. "We spent the entire weekend together, and she was...." Christian trailed into silence when he thought of them in bed.

Bianca raises her bemused eyebrow. "She must be something. He's lost his ability to speak."

"Forty-eight hours of sex with a beautiful woman tends to do that," Lorenzo said.

"So, you think she's beautiful," Christian said.

"She is not as beautiful as you, *amore*, but she is stunning enough to make a man crazy." Lorenzo tilted his chin toward Christian.

"And I think she's done that to him." Bianca and Lorenzo watched Christian, whose mind was full of Toni and miles away.

"I believe you are right, Bianca." Lorenzo paused, dipped into his whiskey, as he considered telling Bianca about the nagging feeling Toni put in his gut.

Lorenzo wasn't in the habit of interfering in Christian's love life. Sometimes, he envied it. What man wouldn't? Christian's life was every man's fantasy. Christian's life was a revolving door of beautiful women who willingly slipped in and out of his bed without the benefit of commitment.

But the nagging feeling at the pit of his stomach Toni put there was something Lorenzo needed to share. Seeing the look in Christian's eyes that told Lorenzo Toni was more than a roll in the sheets for Christian pushed the alarm buttons. Christian was jumping into shark-infested waters, and his sister needed to know. A man's weakness

was the manipulative woman he thought made the room
brighter.

Chapter 10

TONI HAD LEARNED long ago from the best that being too obvious blunted a man's interest, so she waited a few days to return Christian's many calls. Proof that delayed gratification worked was that tonight, Toni sat in Christian's kitchen, watching him expertly make dinner for them.

Beyond the sliding glass doors, the setting sun across the skyline looked like a fiery explosion of russet and gold. A cold winter's wind blew against the double-pane glass, but inside the kitchen with white lacquer cabinets and oversized stainless steel appliances, a cozy warmth hung in the air. Ceiling pot lights bloomed bright and bounced off the cream-tiled floor. Earth, Wind & Fire's "After the Love Has Gone" flowed from speakers.

Toni watched Christian roll and knead the pasta dough on the counter before passing it through the press. The pappardelle pasta made, Christian moved to chop tomatoes, crush garlic, and dice vegetables to make the sauce and assemble the garden salad.

Toni wondered what the man did not know how to do.

Christian was remarkable in bed. Now, he seamlessly made his way around the kitchen. There was nothing sexier than a domesticated man, Toni thought. Then there was how his tall, fit body looked in snug jeans and cotton shirt, which had Toni's heart thudding hard in her chest.

As many thought, Nepotism wasn't why Christian rose to the position of Chief Financial Officer in his parents' company. Christian was a wizard with numbers.

Christian's talents and great looks cast a net far and wide to women of breed, culture, and money. Yet Toni was the woman who sat at the stool in Christian's kitchen, sipping on Cabernet Sauvignon, waiting to be served a home-cooked meal by the most desirable bachelor in the country.

But Toni expected no less. She had been taught the art of luring a man and knew how to have him bend to her will. Tonight was no exception. After dinner, Toni would seduce Christian to his bed. She would please him by doing everything he enjoyed while toying with his emotions to put her plan in motion.

"You're a difficult woman to get a hold of." Christian added crushed garlic, chopped onions, red pepper, and celery to the hot olive oil in the pan. The smell of sautéed garlic and vegetables filled the kitchen.

"I am a busy woman." Toni wore a buttoned-down lavender shirt tucked in at the waist of tight, faded jeans. Her black lace bra was visible through the shirt's sheer fabric. Her very blond, shiny hair fell to her shoulders in waves, and her makeup was flawless. "And is not the chase half the fun, and what makes me desirable to you?" Toni sipped on her wine.

"Some, but it's mostly because I like you." Christian added diced tomatoes and chopped vegetables to the sautéed garlic. He sprinkled salt, pepper, and a pinch of oregano and stirred.

Toni rounded the black granite-topped island and brushed the fire-red kissable lips to his. "I like you too, but remember you must only like. Nothing more." Toni pressed her mouth down on his when he opened it to speak. "Nothing more, Christian," she repeated before again meeting his mouth.

With the silky slide of her lips and tongue on his, he tasted sweet Cabernet. Her kiss set his blood on fire and spread the liquid warmth from his groin to his head. Christian pulled her closer and covered her mouth with his. His fervent kiss made every bone in her body soft and her knees weak, and she pulled away.

"Food first, fun later." Toni's fingertips traced lightly over his face. "Maybe."

The vague response gave him a rush of anticipation and drove him to insanity as intended.

"Is it other men keeping you occupied?" Christian asked the question, taking too much space in his head.

Toni gave him a slow smile and said nothing.

"I hope you like pasta with tomato sauce, a garden salad topped with my salad dressing recipe, and bruschetta." Christian walked to the refrigerator and fished for the charcuterie platter.

Toni picked up a prosciutto-wrapped melon from the charcuterie platter and bit into it. "Sounds *delizioso*."

"It is delicious."

"To answer your earlier question, no, I have not been kept busy by other men. If you must know, I have been busy looking for work." She brought the remaining prosciutto-wrapped melon to his mouth, and he opened wide. "You enjoy cooking."

Christian lowered the heat on the sauce when it began to bubble. "I do. Not as an everyday chore, but as a pleasurable stress reliever or when entertaining a beautiful woman."

Toni turned her wine glass around in little circles on the counter. "I would assume there have been many women that have come through your front door."

Christian's brow winged. "Do I see the green-eyed monster in those big blue eyes?"

"What you hear is curiosity."

Christian smiled broadly. "There have been some women."

Now Toni's brow winged high. "Some."

"Many women." Christian dropped the fresh pasta into salted boiling water and dug out the colander from a bottom drawer. "But none as special as you." He stopped to touch her lips on his way to the sink. "And that is the truth and nothing but the truth."

"Good save. Your mother, she teaches you how to cook?"

Christian shook his head. "Mom was too busy working. Besides, Mom may be an excellent businesswoman, but she is not a cook. Gran babysat Bianca and me a lot. She taught us everything domestic. It didn't take with Bianca, but it did with me. Do you cook?"

"I was never taught. My mother is more of a five-star restaurant-type of woman." Toni watched Christian crush a garlic clove with the knife's blade and toss it with olive oil.

"There's a first." Christian brushed the garlic and oil mix onto four slices of toasted bread, which he removed from the hot oven and topped with chopped tomato and onion. "An Italian mother that's not much of a cook."

Toni thought of the words to describe her mother. "She is not the domestic type."

When Styx's "Lady" segued, Christian watched Toni walk to the laptop to scroll through his music collection. "Play anything you like."

"Your music collection is, I think the word is, eclectic."

"I like pretty much everything." Christian reached for the pot on the stove with gloved hands and flipped the boiling water and the pasta into the colander to drain.

"You have Italian music on here," she said, pleased by the discovery.

"We spend a lot of time in Italy. Gran and Pops live there six months a year, and we have family there." Christian twirled pasta onto two dishes.

"Yes. You are related to the famous designer Carlo Mesi." Toni picked up the charcuterie platter off the counter and followed Christian, carrying the two plates of pasta topped with tomato sauce to the table.

"He's my uncle." Christian scraped back the chair at the table for Toni.

"Yes, I know." Toni slid into the chair, picked up the salmon-coloured napkin Christian had set beneath the cutlery and laid it on her lap. "Your grandfather Salvatore Mesi, who adopted him when he was just a few months old, was the one who started the company and gave it to him."

"Yes, that's right." Christian tossed the salad and brought it and the bruschetta plate to the table. "You know much about us."

"I have read up on you. Remember, I want to write a story about you for my blog." Toni filled their wine glasses while Christian grated Parmigiano-Reggiano cheese over the pasta plates.

"Yeah, about that, I'm working on it. I have to get Bianca's clearance."

Toni thought he was a man who followed the rules. She liked that. "I would love to write a story about you, Christian. You may be an accountant but do not lead a boring accountant's life. Your life is interesting and adventurous."

"I suppose, but it's the only life I know." Christian clinked his glass to hers. "I hope you enjoy the meal."

Toni looked up at him. He was so genuine. She had had many men in her life, and none were as unpretentious or as sincere as Christian.

Toni's fingers lightly tapped on her lap beneath the table as if striking piano keys to deal with the angst rising in her.

Chapter 11

DINNER, AS TONI intended, led to the bedroom and the most incredible sex she had ever experienced. Christian made her blood heat and her nerve endings explode. His skillful hands weren't what filled her and made her feel complete, but his giving her everything inside him was what fulfilled her as no man had.

For the first time in memory, Toni felt loved and cared for by the man beside her. She felt steeped in a beautiful dream that, until Christian, had been just that, a distant dream.

Toni felt golden and bright, and she liked the feeling.

Christian rolled over onto his side and leaned his head on his elbow. In the darkness of the room, he looked at Toni. "I was thinking."

"No thinking." Toni lay on her back with her eyes looking content. "Let us lie here for a moment to catch our breath."

"We're looking for social media managers. Christian moved his fingers in slow circles on her breast. "And you're a social media guru."

"I would not say I am a guru. As Lorenzo pointed out, I have only five hundred followers."

"That's only because you haven't had the proper break. What you need is a leg-up."

"Leg-up? I don't understand those words, Christian."

"What I'm saying is that maybe you'd like to work in our marketing department."

Toni's eyes opened wide, and she turned to Christian. "What are you saying, Christian?"

He toyed with her hair. "We're looking for people for a big project we're working on."

"I do not want you to do me any favours. I earn my way."

"I'm not doing you any favours. We have a position available, and you're a good fit. Anyway, it's there if you want it."

Her eyes, sharp and blue, looked into his eyes. He was dead serious. For a moment, Toni looked at Christian blankly without answering.

"I do not think that is a good idea."

"Why not? You need a job, and we need people." Christian curled the tips of her hair around his finger. "Let me do this instead of sending you flowers tomorrow."

A smile played across her face. "You were going to send me flowers."

Christian lay butterfly kisses down her neck. "A big bouquet of roses. Your favourite."

A smile flickered in her eyes. "They are not my favourite. I wrote it on the blog because roses are relatable to the average female reader."

Christian's slash of dark eyebrows rose in an expression admiration. "See, you'd be perfect as a social media manager. I wouldn't have thought of that."

"That is because you are too…." Toni stopped herself from saying honest and instead said, "Numbers oriented."

"Which only further proves you are perfect for the job." Christian gave her a light kiss on the lips.

"All right, I will email you my resume."

"No need for that." He lost himself in the beautiful tangle of her hair, which smelled like spring flowers.

She looked at him a bit more sharply. "You said you were not doing me a favour." Toni felt his lips on her breast. The sensation weaved itself through her system.

"I'm not. I'll tell HR about you, and because it's coming from me, they'll hire you."

"That sounds like a favour, and I do not…."

Christian rolled on her and crushed his mouth on hers. "I want to do this for you. Let me do this for you."

Toni looked into Christian's eyes. They held beauty and kindness, and Toni thought she was never happier than when she was with him. The pang of guilt hit her hard. "You must not fall in love with me, Christian."

He stared at her intently. "It's too late for that."

Toni sat up in bed. She looked at Christian with a pained look of regret. This wasn't supposed to happen. Or was it? Her head was dizzy. Christian was making things difficult for her. It wasn't supposed to get complicated.

"Why do you do that?" Christian stared down at Toni's piano-playing fingers drumming against her thigh, and she stopped. "I've seen you do it often."

"You do not know me, Christian."

He played his mouth over hers. "I know you like to move your fingers randomly."

"It is a reaction to control my nervousness. What you call a…." Toni dug into her brain for the word, but her clouded mind failed her.

"Do you mean nervous twitch?" Christian said, and Toni nodded. "I make you nervous." Christian linked his fingers through hers. "I'm taking it as a good sign because I didn't think anything made you nervous."

Toni pulled her hand away and hugged her legs tightly to her body. "There is a lot about me you do not know." Things your family would not look positive on. Do not say anything else, Christian," Toni said when he opened his mouth. Pushing out of bed, she reached for the first piece of clothing she came across the floor. Toni shrugged her naked body into Christian's shirt and headed out of the bedroom. "I am going to make coffee. I need coffee." She didn't.

"I'll make it for you."

"No, do not come with me. I mean, you take a shower," Toni suggested because she needed to put distance between them to gather her thoughts.

Chapter 12

TONI FILLED THE coffee machine's reservoir with water, placed the coffee pod into the slot, and set it to brew. In seconds, coffee spurted into the cup below and bathed the room with its scent.

Toni added cream and sugar to her cup and walked to the living room. The morning sun, a sliver of gold peeking through the blinds, cast long shadows on the immaculate living room. Toni slid the blinds open to let the room bloom bright.

Locating the fireplace remote, Toni turned it on. Flames spurted to life, and she felt the heat warm the room. Probing eyes darted around the stylish, minimally furnished room. Christian said an uncluttered home meant a tidy mind.

The living room, furnished with Italian leather and European dark wood, was tiled in shiny, cream-coloured marble. There wasn't a speck of dust, and everything was in its place. Even the colourful pillows on the white leather sofa were neatly stacked.

The man was freakishly neat.

Continuing her scan, Toni's eyes landed on the collection of framed photographs on the baby grand piano. Her fingers trailed across the piano's smooth surface to the family photos of the Sabatinis and Mesis, a tapestry of success, unconditional love, and wealth.

A sharp and unfamiliar pang of longing pierced Toni. Some had everything. Life was so unfair. These people were rolling in money. They lived in grand homes, enjoying every comfort life offered, while she and her mother had to do what they needed to do for their survival.

In the pit of Toni's stomach, a painful knot tightened.

Her mother was all Toni had in her life. They were friends and told each other everything. Honesty was paramount in a relationship was her mother's motto.

The truth Toni and her mother shared was absolute.

It was why her mother didn't conceal Toni's illegitimacy from her. Her mother told Toni about her many affairs, mainly with married men, and that she didn't know who her father was.

Toni's mother had made it clear the affairs were a necessary evil. It was how she financially provided for them. Men—or uncles, as Toni was told to call them— coming and leaving was a part of her existence, and she came to believe, a part of everyday life.

Toni had never felt self-conscious or awkward about her illegitimacy. It was the reality of her life, and she accepted it before she could walk. However, dealing with the inequity life served based on genetic makeup was a different story.

Toni picked up a photo of Christian as a young boy, his grin mischievous and his eyes sparkling with an innocence she had long lost. Shame, heavy and suffocating, threatened to consume Toni. She had infiltrated Christian's home, exploited his trust, and would now profit from his love, all for her mother's twisted desires.

Toni breathed in several times and then let the breath out through her nose.

Calm again, Toni thought of her past few hours with Christian. They spent most of the night rolling hot between the sheets. The man had stamina and knew his way around the female anatomy. His gentle touch and caring manner put every man who had shared her bed to shame. Christian knew how and where to touch her and what to say.

The man was a poet with words, but Toni was better.

Toni was skilled in the art of conversation, seduction, and pleasing a man. Toni already had Christian wrapped around her finger physically and emotionally. Days into their acquaintance, Christian was already crazy in love with her.

Her mother would be proud.

Her mother raised Toni to believe men were tools for pleasure and to be manipulated for profit. Nothing more. That applied to every man, including her father, whoever he was.

Once or twice, Toni thought about seeking her father but quickly dismissed the idea. Looking for her father required turning to her mother for information and money; neither was an option. Besides, the answer might be worse than not knowing. What if her father didn't want to be found or her in his life?

Her mother had shielded Toni from rejection, and Toni wouldn't know how to deal with it. Her mother wasn't perfect, but she raised Toni as best as possible in a loving environment and taught her to be a survivor.

Toni's "uncles" provided well enough, and Toni never lived a paltry existence, but Toni had not lived a life of consistency and stability. Toni had not lived in the luxury she saw in Christian's modern two-story gray brick home with its many windows and curving driveway bordered by majestic pines and Victorian bevelled-glass lampposts.

The walls throughout the house were covered in costly artwork. Toni didn't believe they were originals, but they were expensive nonetheless. Upstairs, there were six bedrooms and four bathrooms. The house overlooked acres and acres of land, which were now blanketed in snow. Toni imagined flowering trees, manicured lawns, and gardens in riotous bloom in the spring.

Toni walked to the picture window. Looking beyond the glass wall, under the glimmer of morning light, she thought she saw a pond or stream running through the property. It was frozen, but she imagined clear water flowing over rocks in the warm months and the animals that came to it to quench their thirst.

Toni had never enjoyed such luxury, but she would now, for her mother's and her sake.

If Toni played her cards right with Christian, she and her mother wouldn't have just to survive. Toni wouldn't have to seduce men and sleep with them to ensure their existence. They would live in the lap of luxury for a long time.

Toni's heart pulsed at the thought.

The buzz Toni had going was replaced with annoyance when her phone rang. Annoyance turned into delight when she read the telephone's screen.

"Where the hell have you been? I've been calling you since yesterday," said the impatient voice at the end of the line before Toni could say anything.

Toni took a long breath, held it, and then let it out through her nose. Calm descending on her, she said, "I've been busy."

"What could keep you from answering my calls?" The caller snapped.

Toni breathed deeper. "Guess where I am right at this moment?"

"How the hell would I know when you don't answer your goddamn phone?" was the abrupt response from the caller.

"I am in his house, in his living room, to be exact." The comment pleased the caller, as Toni knew it would. "He told me to make myself at home while he takes a shower."

The response was a pleased one. "So you spent the night with him"?

"I am spending the weekend with him." Toni's thoughts wandered to the last few hours with Christian, and her smile went wide. Christian skillfully stoked it When she needed her itch scratched and wanted the fire to burn in her veins.

The terse voice at the end of the line jolted Toni back to the present. "Describe his house to me."

"As you guessed, it is huge and spectacular." Toni fell back onto the sofa and stretched her legs. Tucking the cell phone against her shoulder, she described Christian's house in detail. "He has an indoor and an outdoor swimming pool. Two pools." Toni sighed as she answered the caller's next question. "Yes, he is amazing in bed, and yes, I know not to fall in love with him." Toni's mind was going dizzy as she listened to the preaching voice over the telephone.

If lecturing were a sport, Toni thought her mother would be a gold medalist.

"I already said I will not fall in love with him." Toni went silent when her mother set off for her usual lecture.

Toni simulated the piano playing fingers on her thigh. "I know emotions only serve to cloud your mind and will deter me from what I must do. I will do what you want, Mama, and get what you want." Toni hissed between clenched teeth. "Christian has told me he will get me a job at the company." Toni pushed to her feet and crossed to the window.

Toni's eyes were transfixed on the beauty before her. Christian's property was bathed under the radiance of a full sun. The snow cladding the land and the icicles hanging from tree branches radiated a peaceful stillness.

"Christian says I can work in the marketing department on some big social media project they're working on. Working at the company will give me access to information I could not get otherwise. Are you pleased, Mama?"

"I am. Very much so." The excitement over the news had her mother catching her breath. "I told you the dominance of a woman is formidable when she sets her mind."

"You have, Mama." Toni exhaled a breath. "I did good, yes?"

"Yes, my beautiful daughter, you did very well. You will report everything you hear, smell, and see. We'll be financially set for life if we play our cards right. Understood?"

"I do. I love…." The line cut off, and Toni's fingers played faster.

Chapter 13

BIANCA CAME TO a complete stop at the living room door and aimed eyes at the woman standing at the window, seemingly lost in her thoughts. She was barefoot and wore a short man's shirt—presumably Christian's. Her hands were wrapped around the coffee cup as a wisp of steam eased up.

Serena's eyes widened. "Mommy, there's a naked woman in Uncle Chris's living room."

The child's voice made Toni turn from the window. The look on Toni's face was one of genuine surprise as she swept her eyes over the girls standing on either side of the tall, elegant woman. The girl's face bore a resemblance to the woman's. All stared at Toni, including the small dog with large black eyes propped on his rump at the shorter girl's feet.

The intensity of the silence that hung in the air was palpable.

Bianca studied Toni. Her blonde hair was pulled back in a ponytail, with loose wisps of her hair spilling around her delicate face. Although Toni's face was unpainted, there was a robust, healthy glow about her that Bianca surmised was put there by her brother.

"Who are you?" Rosanna gave Toni a cagey stare out of blue eyes as Toni wrapped her arms around her body.

Bianca shushed her daughter with a reproving look. "I'm sorry for the intrusion, but my brother Christian promised to take the girls…."

"And Romeo," Serena jumped in to say, and the dog's tail swished in excitement when he heard his name.

"Yes, and Romeo, ice skating today. He told us to meet him here at nine."

"He is in the shower." Toni pointed her index finger upward and saw the dog raise one eye and then the other as if scrutinizing her. "I am Toni," she said after a prolonged, awkward silence.

Bianca made the connection to the woman from the restaurant. She was a head-turner, as Lorenzo said, and he was right when he told her the woman ticked all of Christian's boxes. The Italian accent was a definite attention-grabber. Bianca could see her brother's upper brain clouded by her, and his lower brain beguiled.

"I'm Bianca. These are my daughters, Rosanna and…."

"I'm Serena, and this is Romeo." The dog barked his hello. "We're babysitting him for Gran while she's visiting the world."

Rosanna rolled her eyes dramatically. "It's dog-sitting, Serena, while Gran's in Italy."

"Right, dog-sitting. I'm hoping Gran gives Romeo to me. She says I must prove that I'll care for him, and I have this whole time. Haven't I, Romeo?" Romeo rose on his hind legs and planted his paws on Serena's thighs. "Uncle Chris is my uncle."

"I think if you call him Uncle Chris, it's assumed he's our uncle, stupid," Rosanna taunted.

"Don't call me stupid," Serena yelled at her sister, and Romeo barked in support.

"Well, you are," Rosanna shot back, and Romeo barked his disapproval.

"Girls, please behave, or neither of you is going ice skating. That includes you, Romeo," Bianca said, and everyone went silent.

"I don't think we are anyway since Uncle Chris is busy." Rosanna's eyes were slitted when she turned from her mother to Toni.

Toni smiled faintly. "I made coffee." She pointed a finger toward the kitchen.

Serena made a little snorting giggle. "We're too small to drink coffee."

"You two go watch television while we wait for your uncle. Go on, Rosie, and take your sister and Romeo." Bianca signalled Rosanna to move along when she started to refuse. "And no taunting your sister or getting the dog worked up."

"Would you like a cup of coffee? I know how to make cappuccino." Toni offered.

"Thank you. Black coffee will be fine." Bianca followed Toni to the kitchen, eyeing her the entire way.

The bright morning sun bouncing off the snow on the patio deck brightened the room. The scent of coffee lingered in the air and mingled with Bianca's perfume.

"I should go change," Toni said when she felt Bianca's eyes on her.

"If it's on my account, don't bother." Bianca unwound her scarf and unbuttoned the black buttons of her white mohair coat. Shrugging out of her coat, Bianca hung it on the back of the barstool pushed against the kitchen island.

Toni gave Bianca a subtle glance over.

Bianca wore a lilac cashmere sweater and slim-fitting jeans. The gold chain around her neck had a diamond at the center of the woven heart. She had gold teardrop earrings and wore an enviable Bvlgari watch with brilliant-cut diamonds on her left wrist. On her wedding finger, she wore a three-karat diamond.

"I do not cook, but I can make you toast with butter if," Toni looked around the clear counters, "I can find the bread and the toaster. Christian keeps this kitchen very neat."

"He always has been a neat freak," Bianca said, sitting on a stool at the kitchen island. "Coffee's fine."

"I can do that." Toni walked to the pantry and fished out a coffee pod. She removed the used pod from the holder and replaced it with the one in her hand. Toni placed a cup under the spout and set the coffee to brew. "Christian did not tell me he was taking your girls skating. I would have … dressed." Toni's tone was apologetic.

Bianca brushed her flowing hair from her face. "He probably forgot. My brother has a brain the size of the universe when it comes to numbers, but that's where it ends. And when he's entertaining a beautiful woman, his head's not thinking straight."

"I am not that, especially how I look right now," Toni replied when she felt Bianca looking her over.

"I'm sorry for staring, but you look familiar. Have we met before?" Bianca took the cup Toni held out to her.

"I do not believe so. I only met Christian and your husband at the restaurant for the first time a few weeks ago. I wanted to write an article on Christian for my blog, hoping it would increase my female followers."

Bianca grinned. "That should be an interesting read."

"Yes, it would be, but I will no longer write it." Toni brought the coffee cup between her hands to her lips and sipped.

Bianca looked at Toni with curiosity. "Why not? You now have far more information than you bargained for."

The flush of pink rose from Toni's neck to her cheeks at the insinuation. "That is not the type of article I want to write, and now that I unwisely … accepted his dinner invitation at his home, I cannot write anything. Having more than dinner with someone you want to use for clicks was not a good idea."

"No, it wasn't," Bianca said, appreciating Toni's candour. "A word of advice. You need to stay focused on your goal—always."

"Those are wise words. I must remember them for the next time. Anyway, now I must find another subject."

"One, you won't consider going beyond dinner at a public restaurant." Bianca pointed out, and Toni acquiesced. For a moment, Bianca stared at Toni as she worked on the idea that had formed in her head. "Maybe I can help you with that."

Toni beamed back. "You are offering Lorenzo for the story. I know he will get me many clicks. Between you and me, I wanted to speak to Lorenzo the day I met them at the restaurant, but he is married. Married men are not my style."

Bianca began to laugh. "Good to know, and no, I'm not throwing my husband as clickbait for the she-wolves to scrutinize. How many followers do you have?"

She glanced sideways at Bianca, then away. "Five hundred."

"It's a start."

Toni didn't mask her surprise. "Really?"

"Sure. Are you a hobby writer or journalist, Toni?"

"I did not study writing in school. If that is what you ask."

"Yes, it is."

"I mostly worked as a secretary or assistant, but many men I worked for wanted too much assistance. If you understand what I mean."

"Unfortunately, I do." Bianca watched Toni's face take on a warm glow, and her eyes brightened as Christian walked into the room.

Bianca spun in her seat to face Christian. His hair was curled with dampness from his shower. His beard was neatly trimmed, and he wore a white shirt, a fresh pair of jeans, and tan loafers. The look on his face was that of a man who had spent a night in sexual bliss.

Christian came to a sudden stop when he saw Bianca. "What are you doing here?"

Bianca rested her arm on the back of the stool and gave him a minute. "And there it is," she said when she saw the recollection come over his face.

"Shit, ice skating."

"The girls are in the living room, my guess, killing each other by now. They have a lot of pent-up energy they need to burn up and are looking forward to spending time with their uncle. So you better not disappoint them." Bianca looked at Toni. "I'm sorry, but he promised them."

Toni swung her eyes in Christian's direction. "You cannot break a promise to your nieces. You must take them ice skating."

Christian threw his hands up in the air, feeling the total weight of Toni and Bianca's stare burning into him. "Yes. Of course. I will. Will you come with us?"

"Pfft, do I look like a winter person?" Toni rolled her eyes.

"Yeah, I didn't think so." Christian reached for the coffee cup in Bianca's hand.

"And I need to go into the office for a few hours," Bianca said.

"I wasn't asking you." Christian sipped on black coffee and winced.

Bianca smiled slightly. "I'll be going now."

"Let me escort you out of my home, sister of mine." Christian stepped aside and waved Bianca through.

"It was nice meeting you, Toni, and you'd be smart not to go out there. It's freezing." Bianca slid her arms into her coat.

"Pfft, as if," Toni said, and both women laughed. "I will be upstairs taking a bubble bath."

"All right, that's enough from the two of you." Irritation rushed to the surface, and Christian made a rolling hand gesture to move Bianca along.

Bianca stopped at the living room to say goodbye to her daughters, and after giving his nieces his assurance he would be taking them skating shortly, Christian walked his sister to the front door.

"She seems to be a keeper," Bianca said.

"Since when have I wanted your approval of my love life?" Christian watched Bianca slip on her boots.

"Since when have you walked me out?"

"Fair point. I'll be there in a minute." Christian called out to the girls when they called for him. "You should enroll those girls in a prep school as soon as possible."

"Or a boot camp." Bianca buttoned her coat and wound her scarf around her neck.

"There's that." Christian picked up Bianca's handbag off the foyer table and handed it to her. "You really like Toni?"

"I do. She seems to be the type that won't put up with your shit." Bianca reached into the handbag for her sunglasses before shouldering it. She watched her brother squirm and waver as he found the best way to ask his question. After thirty seconds, she decided to put him out of his misery. "I'm still looking for an assistant to replace Joshua. I'll give her a trial run. Hopefully, she'll work out and stay on permanently. I'm tired of the temporaries I've had to date."

Christian's face held just enough shock as he stared at Bianca intently. "Wait, how did you know what I was going to ask?"

"She told me about being unable to write the article on you for her blog after sleeping with you. If I know you, and I do, my dear brother," she pinched his cheek, "You're feeling guilty now and want to find her work. Am I wrong?"

Christian simply gaped at her. "You've always said I can't have my bed-friends hired at the company."

"But for this one exception, that policy stands."

"Why is she the exception?" His voice was full of puzzlement. "You make no exceptions. For anyone. Ever."

"Why are you so suspicious? I'm giving her a well-paying job with the offer of permanency." Bianca dug into her coat pocket for her car key and turned to open the front door.

"Because when it comes to business, you're calculating. You don't do favours." Christian stared at Bianca some more. "Why take her on as your assistant? She's interested in social media."

"Because I haven't replaced Joshua yet, and I believe Toni would do a good job."

Christian suspicious eyes studied Bianca. "Nah, that's not it. You're plotting. I know you."

"She's not into social media. It's just something she's trying out. I listen, observe, and pay attention to people. It's something you should do more often, baby brother." Bianca smacked his cheek twice with the palm of her hand. "This is why I'm the CEO, and you are a number pusher."

"No. You wouldn't be this accommodating unless you had a purpose for Toni." Christian didn't like the mischievous smile on Bianca's face as she set her sunglasses on her nose. "I know that look. It's not a good one."

"Tell her to show up for work Monday morning. Have her swing by HR to get signed up on the payroll and get her access card. I'll send them an email authorizing it."

"I'll escort her personally, but I want to know what you plan to do, Bianca. I like this woman. I really like her."

"Keep the girls out as long as you want." She pecked him on the cheek and walked out the front door into the frigid morning air.

"You better not be planning to throw her to any wolves. I'm warning you, Bianca," Christian called out before she pressed the gas, and the wheels of her SUV crunched over packed snow as she drove off.

Chapter 14

TWO HOURS LATER, Romeo, Serena, Rosanna, and Christian returned from skating. Their faces were flush with colour.

Leaning a shoulder against the living room door, Toni watched Christian interact with the girls while Romeo raced around the foyer barking. Christian removed Serena and Rosanna's hat, jacket, and boots and tossed everything over his shoulder, sending the girls into a giggling fit. Christian then shed his leather jacket and wool hat and threw it into the pile as Romeo circled it excitedly, barking.

Christian was the father any child would have fun with, Toni thought.

With a calmer Romeo in tow, the three approached Toni. She wore an oversized pair of track pants and a matching sweatshirt that she had dug out from Christian's closet after her shower. "You had fun," she said.

Drawing to a stop next to Toni, Serena rambled on in between breaths. "We did. It was snowing hard, and Romeo loves it when it snows, and he tried to eat it. Uncle Chris showed us how to skate a figure eight and backward."

Rosanna said, "I already knew how to do all that."

"I didn't, and I only fell...."

"A million times," Rosanna finished for Serena in a taunting tone.

"I did not," Serena shot back, her blue eyes narrowed.

"Rosie, what did I say about teasing your sister?" Christian said.

Rosanna looked up at Christian. "I should do it behind her back to not upset her."

Toni's mouth opened in a stunned O. "Does your sister know this is what you are teaching her daughters?"

"Rosie's going to do it regardless, and so is this munchkin." Christian rubbed a hand over Serena's static flyaway hair. "They're sisters, and it's what siblings do. Eventually, they'll tire of it and become best friends because they're siblings."

Toni opened her mouth and closed it when Serena cut in. "I'm thirsty, Uncle Chris."

"Yeah, me too," Rosanna echoed.

"How does hot chocolate sound? I made some when Christian texted me that you were on the way back from skating. It is on the stove," Toni said.

"With marshmallows. I like marshmallows. The little ones, not the big ones. I like the way they float at the top and how squishy they taste in my mouth," Serena rambled on.

"Come on. I know where Uncle Chris keeps them. I like little marshmallows, too." Rosanna reached for her sister's hand and led her to the kitchen.

"Can Romeo have some? He's probably thirsty, too."

"He can't have chocolate, remember?" Rosanna reminded her sister. "We'll get him water and a treat. I know where Uncle Chris keeps Romeo's treats."

"Okay, come on, Romeo. Rosie's getting you a treat," Serena signalled the dog to follow them, and he happily did.

"See, love is back in the air. It's what siblings do." Christian's slanted a look over his shoulder. Toni wore no makeup, her hair was tied into a messy ponytail, and she looked centrefold-worthy. "By the way, you look great in my clothes." Christian reached for Toni's hand.

"I am not wearing anything underneath," Toni volunteered, and both exchanged a long, pointed look.

"But right now, we have hot chocolate and pizza," she said, the last word loud enough for Rosanna and Serena to hear. "Would you like that, girls?"

Both girls shrieked, "Yes, please, Toni."

"You're going to make the pizza because I'm too tired to cook anything."

Toni laughed, moving her head and making her earrings dangle like wind chimes from her ears. "God invented the telephone and delivery for a reason."

"Yes, of course, stupid me."

They finished an extra-large pepperoni pizza and chased it with brownies. Afterwards, they gathered in the living room around the coffee table and played board games. Romeo stretched out in front of the fireplace and dozed off.

This, Toni thought, was what family was about.

"Why don't you girls play the piano for Toni," Christian poured two glasses of Rémy Martin at the bar and brought them to the sofa.

"You play the piano?" Toni took her glass from Christian.

"Mommy makes us take lessons, and I hate it." Rosanna's eyebrows lifted in mild disdain.

"I like it. I can play Chopsticks and some Twinkle Twinkle Little Star. I know the words, too. Do you know them, Toni? Do you know how to play the piano?" Serena looked up at Toni with her big blue eyes.

"I know the words to Twinkle Twinkle Little Star. It is my favourite song," Toni set her glass down and rose from the sofa.

Serena's eyes went wide. "Mine too. Come and sing it with me, Toni. We can sing together. Uncle Chris, you want to sing with us?"

"No, baby. Uncle Chris can do many things, but singing is not one of them. I'm just going to sit here, sip my drink and listen to the three of you."

"Okay, Uncle Chris. Come on, Rosanna." Serena waved her sister over to the piano.

"I don't want to sing," Rosanna fell back on the sofa next to Christian, her arms crossed on her chest.

"Maybe after Serena and I finish singing, Rosanna, you can teach me how to play the piano. I had some lessons from a friend long ago but would like to learn properly. Will you teach me?"

Rosanna's brows puckered in bewilderment. "You want to learn from me?"

"I do. You are probably very good at playing the piano and an excellent teacher, and I am eager to learn everything you know." Toni's voice held as much excitement as Rosanna's face did.

"I can teach you, Toni," Serena said.

Toni smiled warmly at Serena, taking the girl's face between her hands. "You, *amore*, will teach me to sing. I need a talented singer like you as a teacher."

Serena grinned. "I can do that."

First, they sang, and then Rosanna took Serena's place at the piano bench and spent thirty minutes showing Toni what she'd learned. Christian noticed Rosanna's face light up in wonder like a child's on Christmas day when Toni played five minutes of Swan Lake on her own like a professional.

"You know how to play the piano and play it well, don't you?" Christian whispered in Toni's ear when Rosanna was out of hearing rage.

"I am no Mozart and mostly taught myself, but I play. I took it up because it calms me. Some people drink, and others play video games. I play the piano when I need calming."

Christian drew back slightly and curiously eyed her. "Why pretend you didn't?"

"She is a blossoming young lady, and sometimes it is nice to be cherished and appreciated by an adult." Toni kissed Christian on the lips and walked out of the kitchen, leaving him staring at her in wonder.

Part II

The Middle

By our acts, we create our destiny.

—M.L. Lexi

Chapter 15

TONI STOPPED AT Bianca's office door.

Things had worked out better than Toni expected, swiftly and with little effort. As Bianca's assistant, Toni's reach went deeper into the company than she thought possible. She had access to documents, files, projects, and everything coming down the pike.

Toni didn't need to sleep with Christian, but she didn't see that as a negative. The man was a fantastic lover who pushed all the right buttons in bed. A reasonable certainty is that Toni would continue to let him do so. Also, Christian was a great backup plan if things went south on the job.

The dutiful daughter, Toni, reported everything and anything she saw and heard at the company to her mother through the burner phone she made her buy. Caution was paramount to the success of any plan; her mother stressed often enough, and Toni wasn't leaving any traceable crumbs.

Toni didn't know what her mother was plotting. On a need-to-know basis, Toni never knew what her mother was up to. That was fine with Toni because she would rather not know the details.

Walking into Bianca's office, like a floating aura, Toni felt the influence the woman behind the desk wielded, as she had every time that week. As it always did, Toni's expression turned into awe. Never had Toni imagined a woman at the helm of a multi-billion dollar empire making the decisions that affected tens of thousands of employees worldwide.

The office was remarkable. The view from the tall glass walls was spectacular, and Bianca, in the royal blue tailored blazer with gold button, her hair swept up, looked authoritative and classy.

Toni was mesmerized by Bianca's confidence, capability, and influence. Bianca's decisions affected market trends and generated millions of dollars in sales. And as much clout as Bianca wielded, she was confident, not arrogant, and firm but not aggressive—a new concept to Toni, who grew up believing otherwise of women.

Toni cleared her throat to announce her presence. "You wanted to see me, Bianca. As you asked, I have requested Margie, Carole, and their boss, Suzanne, to meet with you. They should be here in twenty minutes."

Bianca looked up from her papers to meet Toni's gaze. She wore a cobalt blouse with a flowing neckline bow, and the tight pencil skirt showed off generous curves. The pointy pumps with a high heel made her toned legs look longer. Her glossy blonde hair fell around a flawlessly made-up face with fire-red lips.

"Thank you." Bianca waved Toni to the sofa in the meeting area. "I thought we could have a chat before they show up."

"Oh, okay." Toni sat ramrod straight with her knees together and laid the notepad on her lap. "Is everything okay, Bianca?"

"It is." Bianca sat across from Toni. "I haven't had much time to talk to you."

"We talk all the time."

"I mean not work-related." Bianca leaned back in her seat and crossed her slender legs with graceful movement. "You've been here for one month, and we haven't had a decent chat."

"You are very busy. I cannot believe how busy you are. I hope I do a good job for you."

Bianca heard the nervous quiver in her voice. "You have done a great job, Toni. I just wanted to check in to see how you're doing. Are you finding your way around? Is everyone treating you well? Sometimes, being my assistant can cause resentment and jealousy in your colleagues. Especially if you're a friend of Christian's, which I'm assuming people know by now," Bianca said.

"Everyone is very nice. The job is more challenging than I imagined. You work in comparison to my past bosses." Toni watched the smile bloom on Bianca's face. "But I enjoy the work and think I do a good job for you." There was a pause, and Toni nervously played her fingers on the notepad. "I try very hard, and if people find out I am friends with Christian, they do not find out from me. I know this job demands discretion." An earnest look washed over Toni's face.

"I didn't mean they found out through you. I meant Christian. Contrary to popular belief, men love to talk and flash their feathers like a peacock's."

"If Christian is flashing his feathers, I will pluck them one at a time." Toni's lips pressed together into a long, firm line. "I think that is what you call saying the quiet out loud."

Bianca's mouth tipped at the corner. "Please, don't let me stop from plucking. If anything, I encourage it." Bianca's comment made some of Toni's uneasiness wane. "My door's always open if you want to talk."

"Yes, people have told me this about you. Thank you."

"I'm sure you've heard about the big project Margie, Carole, and Suzanne are working on." Bianca got down to the topic she wanted to discuss with Toni. "Not that I'm not always busy, but I will be more so in the coming months. I need this project rolling promptly and seamlessly. Please let me know if you have any suggestions, even doubtful ones. Sometimes, so-called doubtful suggestions turn out to be the best ones."

Toni thought for a moment. "I actually do have what you call a doubtful suggestion. I was not sure if I should...."

"Our company motto is 'Say what's on your mind.' So tell me what you're thinking, Toni." Bianca sat back and waited.

"I have a friend who lives in Beijing. I met her through my blog and then at a bloggers conference."

Staring back at Toni, Bianca said, "They have bloggers conferences?"

"Yes. They are huge. Anyway, my friend has a young daughter, and she is a very popular...." Toni hesitated.

"Please go on, Toni. Say what's on your mind," Bianca encouraged.

"She is a gamer. You know she plays video games. The girl, named Ming, is seventeen years old and one of the top thirty players, and she can be in the top five. Maybe even number one. She is that good, but because she is a girl, she finds it hard to get sponsors." Toni looked up from her kneaded hands to Bianca and was pleased to see her listening intently.

"Go on, Toni." Bianca's words gave Toni the courage to continue.

"I was thinking you could sponsor her. She has many followers on Weibo. That is like Twitter or X for China. It is one of the biggest social media platforms there. I think Ming has over twenty million followers." Toni waited for Bianca's reaction to the impressive number but saw none.

Bianca was emotionless and expressionless when she spoke. "That's remarkable."

"You are impressed?" Toni asked, looking confused when Bianca nodded. "It is hard to tell."

"Sorry, my mother trained me to stifle emotions unless in anger to make a point. As a woman, it works well when you're in a room full of ego-centric men." Bianca could see Toni compartmentalizing the information for future reference. "Anyway, sponsoring Ming fits with the Farfalla code of supporting female excellence and their advancement."

Toni's voice was more robust now. "That is what I thought. I also thought that Lorenzo could design gaming clothes for her and her team, all girls, to wear at the competitions. They get fifty thousand spectators at each competition and millions online. You know kids love to spend money on clothes that make them look, they call it, rad. Gaming is huge, bigger than many mainstream sports right now."

Bianca leaned back in her chair and was silent for a moment. Her eyes were focused on some distant point, and her neutral facial expression was neither enough for agreement nor implied disapproval.

Toni's confidence shattered. "It was a bad idea. I am sorry I mentioned it," she said, her face reddened and her eyes overflowing with disappointment.

The snow was coming straight down in a persistent but gentle drizzle. The sun was intense, and the snowflakes that struck the windowpane melted, leaving streaks as they slid down.

"No, it's not a bad idea. I was working out the angles in my head. We can call the line of gaming wear G@merwe@r, with an at sign." Bianca gestured for Toni to pass her paper and pen and wrote the name.

"That is catchy and brilliant, Bianca," Toni said, intrigued and impressed that Bianca came up with the catchy logo on the spot. Bianca never ceased to surprise Toni.

"We'll, of course, get marketing to review the name. They may come up with a better one."

"I doubt it. You are brilliant, Bianca," Toni said.

Bianca smiled at Toni. "Thank you, but we work as a team, and getting people's input makes us great. We'll have to vet Ming and her family."

"I do not see a problem with that."

"Good because I like the idea of sponsoring Ming and the Farfalla-Mesi name being associated with her platform. Thank you, Toni, this is an excellent idea. I'm glad you brought it up."

Toni's face flushed with pleasure. "Thank you, Bianca."

"I'll have to run it by Uncle Carlo since the Mesi brand will be associated with the project, and I'll speak to Christian, legal, and Lorenzo...." Bianca stopped momentarily, and Toni saw the contemplative look she'd entered into a few minutes ago overtake her again.

Toni fell into the silence with Bianca.

"You should take the lead on the project, Toni," said Bianca after a thoughtful silence.

Toni seemed genuinely surprised by the suggestion and followed it with a long, dramatic pause. "Me? Really?" Toni said when she found her voice.

Bianca nodded. "It's your idea."

For a long fifteen seconds, Toni gaped at Bianca. "I wouldn't know where to begin."

"You begin by assembling a proposal that estimates budgetary, designing, and legal requirements."

Excited energy rose in Toni, and she rose to pace the room. "I do not know, Bianca. As exciting and challenging as it sounds," Toni turned to Bianca. "I love a challenge, but this may be beyond my expertise. I have never worked on anything this complicated. I do not want to let you down."

"You won't, and you wouldn't be working alone. Ah, here comes the cavalry. Come in." Bianca waved Margie, Carole, and Suzanne to join them when they knocked on her door.

Margie sat on the sofa beside Toni, and Carole and Suzanne followed suit. "What's this about the cavalry?"

"I have the first project for your newly installed Product Management Department. I'd like you to assist Toni with the idea she just presented to me, which I'd like to put into motion immediately. It's connected to our Asian launch, and as you can appreciate, time is of the essence."

As the new kid on the block and Christian's bed warmer, Toni expected backlash, but what she heard was "Sure thing, Bianca," from Margie, a "For sure" from Carole, and an "Of course" from Suzanne.

"Thank you," said an overcome Toni. "I appreciate it."

For the first time in her life, Toni felt significant, with purpose, and a part of a team. Until Bianca, until now, the women who came into her life treated her as an adversary and made her feel ordinary. Toni didn't blame them. She slept with their husbands to extort money.

Being treated as an equal and praised felt good. Toni decided this would remain out of her nightly reports to her mother. It would be her secret because some things were best left unsaid and kept from her mother's reach.

"Good, you ladies get to work on the project. Toni, pencil in a weekly update on the calendar from you and the team in my office. I'll get Christian to work out the numbers." Bianca rose, and everyone followed suit. "If working on the project and being my assistant becomes too much, you must let me know, Toni."

"No. No, it will not be too much, Bianca. Thank you to all of you." Toni's face lit up with a grateful smile.

Chapter 16

BIANCA STRAIGHTENED IN her chair and took a deep, calming breath. "That was an internal leak, and it came from legal. Your department, Marty. Aside from the family, no one but you and your staff had details of Bob Klein's lawsuit. No one knew we were digging up more women outside the company he'd sexually harassed. No one but your department knew their names." Bianca's eyes stayed levelled on Marty, who looked like a deer caught in the headlights.

The weight of Marty's distress in the dark eyes behind the thick square-framed glasses was palpable. "I know, but I don't believe they would do anything this egregious." Marty raked fingers through the short, dark hair silvered at the temples.

"And yet Bob Klein's lawyer has filed a request demanding the testimony we have on the women we dug up. Worse, he has their names after we promised them they wouldn't be made public unless necessary. That is egregious, Marty."

Nerves bouncing, Marty paced. "Agreed, and I've launched an investigation to uncover who's responsible for this debacle. Still, I want it on the record that I don't believe it came from my department. You know my team, Bianca. They're professionals through and through."

"Yes, I know them, but you and I know well how money can miraculously compel a silent voice to break their silence." Bianca rose and walked to the window. In the burgundy two-button jacket and knee-length skirt, she epitomized tailored elegance. "These women are the victims, Marty, not Bob."

Bianca thought of all her mother had endured at the hands of Joe Smith, the emotional trauma Isabella internalized and carried for years for an unprovoked event thrust on her. Bianca vividly recalled the fear, loss of dignity, trust in humanity, and guilt Isabella lived with through no fault of hers.

Two decades later, when Isabella was compelled to tell the evil Joe Smith perpetrated on her to her family, the aftershock was Bianca's to absorb when doubt of who her father was became real. Although Bianca refused to acknowledge anyone other than Antonio was her father and dismissed the DNA report, the uncertainty—however minute—stayed with her.

Uncertainty, fear, guilt, anger, and the myriad of emotions that come with sexual assault, which assails your life is no way to live. It wasn't for Isabella, Bianca, or the women who had the misfortune to come in contact with Bob Klein.

"I will not allow Bob to depict himself as the victim, Marty." The bastard would pay, and Bianca would make sure he did.

"I won't either. I can promise you that." Marty sunk his five-nine frame into the guest chair. "I assure you I will get to the bottom of this, Bianca."

Bianca waved Toni in when she poked her head at the door. "What is it, Toni?"

"I am sorry to interrupt, but the chair for The Isabella Farfalla Foundation and her organizers are here, Bianca. Here are the files you will need for the meeting." Toni set the Manila folder containing the report containing the data points she assembled on Bianca's desk.

"Thank you, Toni. Give Marty and me ten minutes before you send them in."

When they were alone again, Marty asked, "Bianca, does Toni have access to your files and information?"

Bianca's response was a contemplative, "Yes, of course. She's my assistant. She has access to everything I work on."

Marty gave Bianca a long look as her eyebrows knit together in concern. "Do you want me to include her in my investigation?"

Bianca shook her head. "Let me think about it."

"Okay, but as your legal counsel, I advise you that we should. It won't hurt."

It would hurt Christian and wouldn't go down well if he learned Bianca signed off on an investigation on Toni, the woman he fell in love with.

"I'll get back to you. Marty, this stays between us," Bianca said in an unalive tone as her mind raced.

"That goes without saying, Bianca." Marty rose and left the office, leaving Bianca deep in thought.

Chapter 17

TONI LOOKED FORWARD to the Friday morning meeting to update Bianca on where they stood on her project. For weeks, Toni worked twelve-hour days, seven days per week. Toni had never worked as hard in her life, and aside from not being able to spend more time with Christian, she enjoyed every minute.

Working for Bianca on The Ming Project was an invaluable experience for Toni. For the first time, Toni worked toward a worthy, selfless goal and, in the process, realized she was capable and skilled at something other than seducing men. It taught Toni that she didn't need a man to exist and that she was a capable woman who didn't need to rely on a man to exist. Toni learned she could sustain herself doing something she was good at and enjoyed.

Toni owed her awakening to Bianca and the women at the table.

Toni looked around Bianca's meeting table at Margie, Carole, and Suzanne, the women she now considered more than colleagues. Toni considered them her friends.

Margie was bright as a whip. She had strawberry-blonde hair and vivid blue eyes and was as good-natured as she was pretty. Margie was the free spirit of the group, whereas Carole was the glue that bound the group. Carole's hair was burnished, glossy brown, and her dark eyes reflected her intelligence. Then there was Suzanne, the research whizz. She had a flaming red halo that framed an alabaster face flecked with freckles. Her eyes were dazzlingly green, and confidence was her middle name.

As different as the women were in appearance, they had one thing in common: work ethic. Margie, Carole, and Susanne worked hard and were goal-oriented, independent women. And Toni considered each one a friend.

With a sparkle in her eyes, Toni gave Bianca an update on The Ming Project. "With the help of the ladies at this table, Ming and her mom have been vetted and passed the Farfalla sponsorship requirements with flying colours."

"While we were at it, we also vetted all the members of Ming's team, just in case you'd like to consider sponsoring them," Carole added.

Margie went on when Bianca said nothing. "We, along with Toni, spoke to marketing about the g@merwe@r brand you came up with, which, by the way, we all thought was brilliant. Anyway, they loved both the name and the unique spelling. These are the three designs they came up with." Toni spread the sketches on the table before Bianca.

"This one was the favourite of the group." Toni pointed a manicured finger at the design, in an essence font with lowercase letters and the at signs painted red. "The symbol for the g@merwe@r brand, upon your approval, Bianca, will be a red ampersand with the word g@merwe@r arched above it. Red is the most popular colour associated with gaming," Toni pointed out.

Carole continued. "We've submitted the request to the legal department to trademark the name for The Farfalla

Company. They should have it registered in the coming month, and we'll submit the logo once you approve it."

Toni picked up from there. "We met with Lorenzo and Joshua to discuss the possibility and timeline for putting g@merwe@r garments on the market. As it turns out, Joshua is a big gamer himself, and for his last school assignment, he designed a collection of gaming outfits."

"A visionary our Joshua is." Bianca flipped through Joshua's pencilled designs.

"Lorenzo will present the final designs to you once he's had a chance to review them and tweak them if necessary for your approval," said Carole.

"Those are the key points. Before you, the report outlines the many other steps we addressed, such as timelines for pressers and promotions campaigns to expedite the project as quickly as possible," Suzanne said.

While Bianca read the charts to keep her fingers from drumming, Toni busied herself by refreshing everyone's coffee and serving croissants that no one had asked. Toni also added a side order of individual butter, strawberry jam servings, and cutlery to the dishes.

"This looks great. As a newly installed department, I'm very impressed with how quickly you've turned this information over, how thorough you've been, and how much you've accomplished in a few weeks," Bianca said when she finished reading the report.

"These ladies are not only great to work with, Bianca, but they know what they are doing." Toni glanced over at Margie, Carole, and Suzanne.

"I agree. If anyone can get this done, I believe it's you ladies. It's good to know I can expect great things from your department." Bianca picked up her cup of coffee and sat back in her chair.

"Thanks for the vote of confidence, Bianca," Margie said.

"You're welcome. All we need now is the financials."

Suzanne said, "Christian's working on it. He has a lot on his plate."

"He always does. I'll push him along." Bianca reached for the croissant on her plate, split it open, and spread a thin layer of strawberry jam. "I need his forecast to determine the sustainability aspect of the program. Great work, ladies."

"Thank you, Bianca." Suzanne beamed a prideful smile. "If there isn't anything else, we won't take up any more of your time."

"No, there isn't anything else, but I would like you to stick around for a few more minutes, and Toni, I'd like you to stay to take the minutes of our next meeting. Come, join us," Bianca said when Marty walked into the office in perfectly pleated gabardine pants, black, a silver shirt, and a matching tie. "The subject of this impromptu meeting is Bob Klein's sexual harassment lawsuit."

At the mention of Bob's name, Toni watched Margie, Carole, and Suzanne's spine stiffen and felt the mood in the room turn sombre. Looking from Margie to Carole to Suzanne, a complete understanding crossed Toni's face.

Chapter 18

TONI BROUGHT THE plates of pork chops and mashed potatoes Christian made for dinner to the table and sat. She hadn't changed and was wearing her work skirt and blouse. Her feet were snuggly warm in a pair of fuzzy slippers.

"He is suing the company for a lot of money and his accusers, Margie, Carole, and Suzanne, for defamation. How can this … this … Bob Klein do that? He is the one who stole so much from them because he could not keep his tiny, wrinkled dick under control." Toni's hair pulled back, her blue eyes seemed bigger as anger spit out of them.

Christian countered Toni's pulsing anger with calm. "Don't think about it. Bianca, Marty, and our legal team are handling it. Believe me when I say you don't want to go up against Bianca in this instance." Christian picked up the salad bowl and brought it to the table. "My sister can be one scary bitch when you cross her or hurt the people in her orbit, and this is something close to her. If I know Bianca, she'll win this war."

Christian wore jeans and his trademark white shirt, with the sleeves rolled to the elbow. His hair was mussed just the right way.

"They are such nice girls and too young to deal with something like this." Toni brought up her legs on the chair and circled them with her arms. "They will never trust another man. He has stolen so much from them. It is a heavy burden to carry with you all of your life, and this shrivelled-up excuse of a man did that. *Grande stronzo*."

Big turd was what Christian, too, would call Bob Klein. Still, he was taken aback by the words delivered by Toni with emotion and tinged with fury.

For a moment, Christian's mind raced. "Are you speaking from first-hand knowledge?"

Toni shook her head and saw Christian's visibly distressed expression relax. "Not me." She looked up, her eyes full of anger. "I would never allow a man to do that to me."

Christian felt a deep sense of relief, and he covered Toni's hand with his. "That's very good to know, but you know someone affected by such an experience."

Toni rested her head on her updrawn knees and slipped into silence to gather the strength to say what came next. Christian rode the silence with her to give her time to collect her thoughts.

"My mother. She was stalked and raped by the man obsessed with her. After lots of therapy, she could get on with her life, but the trauma from the experience never left her. I…." Toni hesitated, and they were quiet for a while again.

For a moment, there was only the sound of the crackle of flame from the fireplace. Christian rode the silence with her to give her time to collect her thoughts.

"You don't have to tell me anything if you don't want to, but I'm here if you need a listening ear," Christian said after the floating silence.

"There are times I think he is my father." Toni surprised herself with the revelation she had buried inside her until now.

Toni had never spoken about her dark secret with anyone for fear of their reaction, but Christian didn't disappoint her. Christian's expression wasn't pity or repulsion. He didn't judge or offer emotional kindness. Christian's expression was one of affection.

Christian leaned in and kissed Toni tenderly. "The food's getting cold."

"Did you hear what I said, Christian?"

Nodding, Christian uncorked the bottle of Pinot Noir and poured wine into their glasses.

"What would your parents, Bianca and Lorenzo, say if they learned I was a bastard child? The product of rape?" Toni's voice wavered.

Christian sat back in his chair, looked her in the eye and saw raw pain, heartache, and fear. It broke him but kept his expression neutral.

"You come from a perfect family, with good breeding, with so much love."

Christian reached for the bamboo fork and spoon and transferred the salad from the bowl to their dishes. "No family is perfect. Everyone has skeletons in their closets."

"My skeleton is shameful, revolting, and appalling." Toni looked away.

Christian slid his fingers under Toni's chin and turned her face to meet his gaze. "My family wouldn't judge where you came from or your genetic makeup, but who you are today. Besides, it sounds as if you don't know for sure," Christian said.

Toni shook her head. "I do not. Except to tell me what happened to her, Mama did not want to discuss it. It is too painful for her."

"Eat. The food is getting cold, and you don't want to upset the chef. I hear he's temperamental," Christian said to bridge the awkward moment.

Toni smiled thinly and cut into her pork chop. "My compliments to the chef. This is delicious."

"Do you wish to find your father?" Christian asked, watching her idly run her fork through the potatoes.

"I am scared to open myself to more disappointment," Toni admitted.

Christian brought his glass to his lips and sipped. "When you're ready, I'll help you."

Surprised by Christian's words, Toni sat back and stared at him wide-eyed. "You would do that?"

"I would." Christian cut into his pork chop and brought a generous piece to his mouth. "But only when you're ready. It's a big decision, and you must be mentally prepared to deal with what you find or don't find."

Emotion choked Toni. She hadn't met anyone like Christian. Until Christian, the men in her life took as much from her as she took from them. Tit for tat was the extent of her relationships. Until now, the arrangement worked because emotion played no part in the equation.

"Never fall in love with your mark or any man. It only clouds your judgment and ends up breaking your heart. You must be in control, always. Women, not men, control the tide of life and men's hearts. It's impossible to do that when you become emotionally involved." Since Toni could walk, her mother had drilled these words into Toni's head.

Toni was falling in love with Christian. At least, that's what Toni thought the clutch at her heart meant.

Toni kissed Christian on the cheek. "Thank you."

Christian set his fork and knife down on the plate. "Not knowing who your father is was why you told me not to fall in love with you. Right? Did you think I was so shallow?"

Toni didn't answer him.

Christian looked deeply into Toni's eyes. The sad blue eyes staring at him held secrets he hoped she would eventually feel she could share with him or, at the least, find the answers she needed.

Christian sighed under his breath. "Let's change the topic. Update me on your project. Bianca is pushing for me to work out the numbers for you."

That made Toni smile, and she told Christian what she and her team had presented to Bianca at the morning meeting. Toni forgot her sadness in the telling, and in between pork chop bites, she described the g@merwe@r logo and its design.

"That's a great idea, Toni. All of it, the sponsorship, the design, and the g@merwe@r name, is great." Christian cleared the dishes off the table and plated two pieces of cherry-topped chocolate cheesecake.

"Bianca came up with the name on the spot. She fell into something like a trance. At first, she scared me, but seconds later, she blurted out the name she came up with completely out of the blue."

"Yes, the trance. She's done that since we were kids. She'd do the blank out." Christian made quote signs with his forefinger around "blank out." "Seconds later, she'd devise the perfect excuse to get us out of trouble. She got it from Mom."

Toni watched Christian pour espresso coffee into two cups. "It is a treat to watch her work and listen to her. She makes difficult decisions that would make anyone struggle seamlessly and on the spot. She decided to pursue the project after I presented it to her. I never imagined she would accept my idea, let alone consent there and then. I figured I must wait weeks or months for the green light. That is not the case for Bianca. She decided I should lead the project on the spot and created the logo right there."

Christian grinned at Toni.

"What?"

"It seems like you have a crush on my sister."

"Respect and admiration is what I have for Bianca."

Toni sat on Christian's lap. "I have a crush on you." Toni sat on Christian's lap. "I have a crush on you."

Christian looked into the clear blue eyes. "How much of a crush do you have on me?"

Toni ran her finger through the cheesecake and brought it to his lips. "I can show you how deep my crush for you goes now."

Christian opened his mouth to let Toni slide the cheesecake-laden finger between his lips. "I'm up for that," he said.

"Good," Toni said, lifting her skirt above her thighs and straddling him. "Before I show you how much of a crush I have on you, you must promise me something."

"Anything. Anything at all."

Toni gave him a playful smile when she ran her finger through the whipped cream on the cheesecake again and placed it between her lips. "You will put the numbers together for Ming's sponsorship and the project to present to Bianca."

"I'll do it first thing next week." Christian felt her teeth bite on his earlobe.

"Tomorrow. I want Bianca to have the information by Monday morning." Toni nibbled on his ear and felt his swift response to the bolt of heat she shot through him.

"Oh, Christ!" He couldn't keep his heartbeat from racing if he forced it. "We have the gala tomorrow."

"That is not until tomorrow night." Her mouth was a breath from his.

His face was flushed, and his breath was coming shorter. "Tonight. I'll work on it tonight."

"You are going to be very busy tonight." The feel of her hands unbuttoning his shirt electrified his skin.

Christian let out a long, hopeful breath. "Oh, lucky me."

Toni stopped unbuttoning his shirt. "But only if you promise to work on my numbers tomorrow morning for me to review."

"Saturday morning it is," Christian vowed.

"That is better." Toni tugged her blouse up and away.

"You're very good at this."

She snapped open the catch of her bra, thinking that years of experience tended to do that.

"For the record, you're as brilliant as Bianca. The Ming Project was your idea," he said, yanking her bra off and tossing it over his shoulder.

Chapter 19

TONI SURVEYED THE multitudes of men and women gathered at Roy Thomson Hall for The Isabella Farfalla Foundation, which benefited women and children's organizations. Over the years, Isabella's foundation helped hundreds of single mothers launch successful businesses and rise out of difficult situations to become sustaining individuals. The foundation built children's hospitals, schools, and roads in third-world countries.

Prominent men in tuxedos and women in flowing gowns and impressive jewels, their delicate perfumes scenting the air, came to flash their worth. Sipping on Cristal or fifteen-year-old single malt scotch, they mingled and traded stories of their recent takeovers and fiscal accomplishments. Many of the attendees knew each other. Money, like royalty, didn't delineate far from their roots.

Toni spotted the CEO of the largest Canadian automotive company exchanging notes with the president of the biggest cell phone provider. In green and lilac silk, their wives flashed the mandatory blindingly white gala smile. Toni thought her smile would be as bright if the emeralds and rubies dangling from their ears, tucked-in necks, and wrists hung from her.

Black and white liveried waitpersons served tall flutes of Cristal and amuse-bouche, which Toni learned were bite-sized hors d'oeuvres. Big money ate small. Music from the cello quartet softly floated. The many bars throughout the venue served Scottish and Canadian single malt whiskey, French wines, and Spanish and Belgian beers.

In a few minutes, the bell would sound, and everyone would head into the performance hall to watch Michael Bublé, Andrea Bocelli, Celine Dion, and for the rockers, Rush.

Membership had its privileges.

At night's end, The Isabella Farfalla Foundation would net millions in donations. As much as Toni despised the rich, it was hard to hate them when she was in their midst and relishing every minute.

Toni eyed Christian as he made his way from the bar toward her, a glass of whiskey in one hand and a wine in the other. Christian rocked the James Bond look in the black tuxedo with silk lapels, ribbed white shirt, and black bow tie. His stubble was trimmed, and his dark curls looked stylishly windblown.

Toni saw every female eye turn to Christian. Some tactfully eyed him, while many brazenly gaped like cougars at mealtime. Toni walked to Christian and brushed her lips with his. Hooking her arm through his, Toni telegraphed her message loud and clear: he was there with her, and they were leaving together at the night's end.

"She certainly has her hooks in him," Lorenzo said, watching the interplay.

"I don't blame her." Bianca threaded her hand through the crook of Lorenzo's elbow. He looked handsome in his white tuxedo jacket and black pants. "Lots of cougars here tonight."

Lorenzo surveyed his wife with a marvelling eye. Bianca looked a vision of grace and beauty in the blue trumpet gown with thin straps he designed for the event. Bianca's hair pulled back in a chignon, brought out her delicate face and pink-painted lips. At her ears and neck, she wore diamonds. He could smell her scent over every woman in the venue.

Bianca was the only woman Lorenzo adored. He had from the moment Carlo introduced them. When Lorenzo set eyes on Bianca, he knew she was the woman he wanted to share his life with.

Lorenzo, however, believed that was a pipe dream. Bianca was the daughter and heir to the Farfalla fashion empire, and he was a broke, inexperienced designer whose parents were sheep farmers. The only thing of value to Lorenzo's name was the acre of land he inherited from his parents on their death.

Although Bianca wasn't a spoiled brat—Isabella and Antonio made sure of that—she led a life of privilege one Lorenzo could only dream of.

Raised on a farm knee-deep in sheep manure, Lorenzo attended public school, not the fancy schools Bianca had. The Mesi Scholarship Program allowed Lorenzo to attend design school and later be employed by Carlo Mesi.

Bianca was opinionated, stubborn, and infuriating. She was her own woman with an inner strength that threatened the privileged men in Bianca's circle. It didn't threaten or discourage Lorenzo. It drew him to her.

Bianca didn't give Lorenzo a second glance, but that didn't discourage him. Lorenzo persisted because any woman worth her salt was worth pursuing.

Lorenzo was Carlo's protégé and owed him his education, training, and livelihood. As indebted as Lorenzo was to Carlo, after meeting Bianca, he asked him to put in a good word with Isabella. Carlo did. Carlo hated to lose his up-and-coming designer, but losing him to Isabella was better than losing him to the competition.

Lorenzo left Milan for Canada to work under Isabella's tutelage. Whether through divine intervention or Isabella's, Lorenzo caught Bianca's eye. In time, Bianca chose Lorenzo over the many suitors crowding her life. Now, twelve years married, Bianca still mesmerized him and stoked his fire as she did on their first encounter.

"It is nice to think I can still catch their eye and kindle jealousy in you," Lorenzo said.

Bianca pecked him on the cheek. "You will always have my eye, but I hate to disappoint on the jealousy thing. I'm not jealous. I know women better than you do; those women are vipers in designer clothes and Botox." Bianca pasted the required smile when Galen and Gayle walked past her. "Thank you for coming and for your support."

After shaking the Westons' hands, Lorenzo said, "Those vipers can hiss as loud as they want. I have eyes only for you, *amore*." Lorenzo reached for two flutes of champagne when the server walked by and handed one to Bianca.

Bianca gave Lorenzo an arched look. "Seems you only have eyes for Toni right now."

Lorenzo turned his gaze from Toni to Bianca. "I was admiring my one-shoulder with the chapel train Chiffon dress. Fuchsia suits her colouring perfectly, doesn't it?"

Bianca's eyes glinted with amusement. Only her husband would be more interested in the dress than the curvy woman with firm breasts spilling over the sweetheart neckline.

"Yes, you chose well for her. She looks stunning." Bianca leaned in to peck Kitty Rubinov's cheek and accepted her husband's hand. "It's lovely to see both of you tonight. I appreciate your support."

"You look stunning, Kitty. May I ask who you are wearing tonight?" Lorenzo said in jest of the Farfalla black lace original gown he designed for her.

"Oh, you," Kitty said, gently tapping his arm.

"If you weren't already married," Lorenzo said with a mischievous wink when her husband turned to shake hands with the men who walked up to him.

"You're a rascal." Kitty's smile spread wide as she walked away.

"Toni is a very beautiful woman, and she looks like she belongs here," Lorenzo pointed out when the Rubinovs were out of hearing range.

"Yes, it does look that way." Bianca blew an air kiss at the Giannottis, who waved from the top of the stairs.

"Would it be impolite to say I do not trust her?" Lorenzo felt guilty at finally saying what he had wanted to say aloud for some time.

Bianca shook her head. "I got the same feeling the first time I met her. I'm not sure what it is about her, but she set off my warning bells. And she looks so familiar, but I still can't place her."

Lorenzo looked at Bianca. "With all your suspicions, why did you hire her, and as your assistant nonetheless?"

Bianca's eyes never left Toni as she said, "In the words of the great Sun Tzu, 'keep your friends close; keep your enemies closer.' Her working for me helps me keep an eye on her."

"I assume you have not mentioned this to Christian?" Lorenzo brought the glass to his mouth and sipped on champagne.

"No, and you won't either. At least not until I have proof."

"You better make it sooner than later. He displays all the telltale signs of a man falling in love."

Bianca replied, "I know. I feel terrible. The first time he's serious about the woman in his life, I get a cagey feeling about her. For Christian's sake, I hope my gut is wrong,"

Chapter 20

SOME DAYS, INSTINCT and speculation when making decisions with unpredictable outcomes were all Bianca had, all she could rely on. This was the case as Bianca read Christian's detailed report With Toni anxiously watching.

Flipping from page to page, studying Christian's detailed forecast and risk assessment, Bianca tried to envisage and predict. Christian was thorough, but Bianca still worked through the data to anticipate every eventuality. Investing in a program she knew little about in China, a country she knew even less about, was an unpredictable venture. However, the two million dollar investment and subsequent ten Christian suggested for The Ming Project were a necessary expenditure.

Twelve million dollars to safeguard the unveiling of the Farfalla-Mesi boutiques in China, which stood to make half a billion dollars in the first ten years, was a small price to pay. Aside from that, Bianca determined the expense was inconsequential in proving to her mother and everyone in silent judgment that she was a capable CEO and the right choice to carry on the Farfalla legacy.

Bianca was her mother's daughter. Resolve and a determination to succeed were what she was made of.

Bianca's initial plan to use Toni's blog to publicize Bob Klein's assault on her employees and weed out other victims—where there was one, there were many—morphed into something bigger when Toni brought Ming to her attention. Bianca's strategy changed then. Business was a chess game. Adapt to the play, be three moves ahead of your opponent, or you were dead in the water.

Bianca immediately saw the opportunity in Ming and her millions of followers. Ming's reach was extensive in Asia, where Bianca anticipated Bob would attempt to thwart the launch of the boutiques he'd brought about.

Bianca's guilt for not reading Christian in on her plan hung around her like an albatross, but she couldn't trust him to keep her plan a secret. Christian was getting too close to Toni, and Bianca couldn't risk him telling her and jeopardizing her plan.

A difficult but inevitable decision Bianca had to make.

Bianca was getting the first taste of many unfavourable decisions she would make as the company's head. Bianca didn't think she would be put in the compromising position so soon after stepping into the role and not in a situation where Christian was involved. Bianca didn't like it, but complex and sometimes detrimental decisions were an occupational hazard and a part of the job.

Shifting in her seat, Bianca reached for the pen on her desk. She looked up at Toni, standing on the opposite side of the desk with a hopeful look. Toni wore a flowing teal blouse and pumpkin-orange pencil pants. Her hair was bound into a twirl. As always, Toni's lips were fire-red, and her makeup was airbrushed to perfection.

"The numbers look good. Twelve million dollars is a reasonable investment," Bianca said, putting pen to paper and signing off on the project.

Toni's smile was full of shocked disbelief. "Really?"

Bianca returned Toni's smile. "Yes. What I've read leads me to believe gaming is a growing and profitable market with substantial growth potential and appears to be the future wave."

Toni's brows pressed together in what looked like puzzlement. "You read up on gaming?"

Bianca nodded. "I make it a point to educate myself on the projects I'm considering investing a substantial amount of money into. It wouldn't be prudent of me to infuse money, personnel, and time into a project simply because we can afford to. I had the research department compile a report on Ming and gaming. It turns out a couple of my researchers are familiar with Ming or Beelzebobbi666. Catchy."

Toni's mouth lifted at one corner. "It is gaming. It is—what is the term?—a different animal."

"Yes, it is. I found that out. Research indicates that there are over five hundred million Asian Pacific esports players. Forty percent are female, and gaming generates a staggering yearly revenue in the billions of dollars. Based on that, I'd say this project will be a profitable venture with good returns."

Toni was in awe at the information Bianca tossed from memory. Contrary to what Toni's mother led her to believe, unparalleled success and great wealth didn't come by chance. It came through hard work, knowledge, dedication, and vision. Bianca was a combination of all four, and Toni's respect for her boss grew tenfold.

"Thank you for bringing this to me, Toni. Well done," Bianca said.

Bianca's praise surprised Toni and robbed her of speech. Taking a moment to steady herself, Toni fixed her eyes on the middle distance.

The sky was a brilliant blue, cloudless, bright with sunshine. Spring was showing her face, and trees were sprouting green. Toni watched a gaggle of Canada geese, the first of the season, wing across the sky free, resolute, unwavering, and intent on finding their home. On Lake Ontario, the first boats of the season sailed on calm water.

"It is me who should thank you, Bianca, for believing in me," Toni said when she was in command of herself again.

"My mother taught me long ago that a company is only as good as its employees make it. Listening, encouraging, and praising good ideas when your employees raise them is the hallmark of a successful company. I believe, as my mother does, in supporting excellence."

Toni's cheeks flushed. "Oh, I am not 'excellence,' and you determine whether it is a good idea."

"There is that, but it's a team effort, and you shouldn't underestimate yourself, Toni. I would never have known about Ming if it weren't for you. If it wasn't for you, I wouldn't know about gaming or devised the idea for g@merwe@r." When Toni didn't respond, Bianca continued. "Christian estimates the project will pay back on investment in a year and make money shortly after. If that's the case, you will receive a bonus based on profitability."

Toni's knees weakened, and she had to get off her three-inch heels. She sat.

"I'm glad you got Christian to work on it this weekend. I wasn't expecting the report for at least another week. You do have the magic touch with my brother." The comment whipped more colour into Toni's face. Bianca handed Toni the signed paperwork. "This is now officially your live project. Let Suzanne, Margie, and Carole know. They will help you navigate the maze of departmental personnel to get it off the ground. Any project has many moving parts, and we want to get this done right." There was a pause, a moment of silence, as Toni let that sink in. "You can do this, Toni. I believe in you. If I didn't, I wouldn't put you in charge of the project."

Toni was entrusted with a multi-million-dollar project. Before Bianca, no one had entrusted her with anything, let alone something so massive, so important.

Toni let out a long breath. "You don't know me, Bianca."

Bianca crossed to the coffee machine, tall and elegant in a mossy-grey single-button jacket, ankle-high pants, and black slingbacks. She poured two cups.

"I know you have a great idea," Bianca said, handing Toni the steaming cup of coffee. And I know you're more familiar with this gaming thing than I am."

Confidence bestowed on Toni was a new and extraordinary feeling for her. No one—not even her mother—had made her feel as accomplished as Bianca. Toni liked the remarkable feeling.

"Ming will want to hear the good news. You should call her," Bianca said.

Toni shook her head. "You should be the one to tell her."

Bianca took her seat behind her desk. "How about we call together?" Bianca typed on the laptop, what time is it in Beijing? "Well, maybe not now. It's 3:58 a.m. in Beijing.

"I do not think she minds if we wake her up to give her such good news. Ming is going to be super excited, and so is her mother. This will give her what she needs to put her on the map. I will get her telephone number."

Toni walked to her desk and returned with a folder and her cell phone in hand a few minutes later. She turned the folder over to Bianca. "I found it on my desk. It is from Marty."

Bianca flipped the folder open. "It's about the Bob Klein lawsuit. I'll read it later. Let's make the call." Bianca watched Toni bite her lip as if considering confiding in her. "What is it, Toni?"

"I was thinking…."

"Spit it out, Toni."

"I would like to write an article about Bob Klein on my blog. I know I have only a few readers, but I want to write it for Margie, Carole, and Suzanne. I believe they need a voice to tell their story, and I want to help them do that."

Bianca rose and followed the path of the elongated beam of sun sprawling across the office floor to the window. Sipping coffee, Bianca was silent momentarily and thought how pleased Marty would be to see her plan working out perfectly.

Bianca swivelled her head to Toni. "It's a lovely thought, but I'm afraid that's not possible. Working for the company, and as my assistant nonetheless, makes it impossible for you to broadcast anything about an ongoing lawsuit against the company. It will come back to us."

Looking disconsolate, Toni absently picked up her discarded coffee and sipped. "I did not think I could, but I need to do something for my friends. They have been so nice to me and helped me so much." It hit Toni then, and she sat up straight. You said it could not come directly from me."

And there it was, thought Bianca. "That's right."

"So it may come from someone else."

"What are you thinking, Toni?" Bianca said, hoping Toni was heading in the right direction.

"I get someone, a follower, to post a comment on my blog." Toni rose, took a few steps, and turned to Bianca. "It would be anonymous. We will use a VPN that routes traffic through encrypted servers and networks through several countries to ensure they cannot trace the source. The commenter will mention she heard rumours about Bob Klein, who works at the company I work at, is alleged to be a sexual predator. In the comment, she will warn me to stay away from him." Toni's plan was more than Bianca bargained for. Bianca looked at Toni and held the look for a moment. "It is a bad idea. I am sorry I brought it up."

Bianca walked to the sofa and sat. "No, it's not a bad idea. I didn't understand any of the technical aspects you mentioned. It's as if you were speaking in a foreign geek tongue. I did understand the logistics of your plan, however. Are you sure you want to do this?" Bianca held Toni's gaze.

Toni nodded. "I am sure."

Bianca leaned back and, drinking the last of her coffee, gave Toni a long stare. "If you do this, I can't be connected. You'll have to do it on your own."

Knowing what Bianca said was true, Toni acquiesced. "Margie, Carole, and Suzanne are my friends." They were Toni's first female friendships, and she enjoyed being a part of the sisterhood. "They are very nice ladies who do not deserve what happened to them. I want to do it for them." Toni's voice, laced with passion, was raw and real.

"Fair enough, but you can't let anyone in the company know what you're up to. Not Margie, Carole, Suzanne, no one, Toni."

The inference to keep Christian in the dark came through loud and clear. "Understood. This conversation will remain between you and me, and I will deny we ever spoke of this if I am asked."

"You're my assistant, and I will protect you if it comes to it." Bianca offered, and Toni gave her a grateful nod. "You're on the right track to get a follower to comment on your blog. Preferably someone outside of the country who can't be prosecuted. Better yet, someone who will make it difficult to track herself down," Bianca said.

"I can make that happen."

"You may respond to the comment in a general way. Do not use names or imply that you know firsthand the situation or volunteer information about the case."

"I understand."

"All right then. I'll leave it with you, and we will not speak of this again. Now, let's call Ming to give her the good news that we're sponsoring her and her team."

Toni's reaction was one of disbelief. "All four girls?" Toni's eyes were luminous.

Bianca nodded. "They're a team, as we are, and I couldn't in good conscience sponsor only Ming."

Bianca's generosity had ulterior motives, but rightly or wrongly, it was the course to take.

Chapter 21

WHEN TONI LOOKED at the caller's name on her phone screen, the thrill from her conversation with Bianca was replaced with irritation. Her mother had a knack for ruining everything. Toni moved to decline the call but decided to answer when she figured her mother wouldn't stop calling her.

"I cannot speak right now. I am at work," Toni whispered into her cell phone. Her fingers tapped the flat of her desk in a quick, progressive motion.

"You haven't taken my calls in the past few days. I have you on the phone now, and we're talking." Her mother demanded.

Toni rose from behind her desk and entered the storage room, closing the door behind her. "I have been busy. I work for a living now. Something you do not know anything about."

Her mother let the clipped comment pass. "You're being evasive. What are you hiding from me?"

Toni took a calming breath. "I am hiding nothing.

"You're my daughter, and I know you well. You're hiding something."

"I am hiding nothing," Toni repeated, her fingers drumming quietly on her thigh. "I have nothing to report."

"A week has passed, and you have nothing to tell me? I told you to call me every night. Have you become too important to talk to your mother?"

Toni heard wine poured into a glass, followed by a bottle slamming onto the table. "I am not lying, Mama. I truly have nothing to report."

"I guess spending time at galas, rubbing elbows with the rich and famous, take up too much of your time."

In panic mode now, Toni's mind raced, and she scanned the storage room, looking for the cameras. "How do you know this?"

"I know a lot of people. I have my contacts."

Toni's telephone pinged. She opened the text message and viewed the images. "*Gesù Cristo!*" Toni saw herself in the one-shoulder gown Lorenzo had chosen for her, standing next to Christian with a flute of Cristal in her hand. The second image was of Toni straddling Christian at the kitchen table. The many more that followed were a timeline of her life over the past few weeks. Toni fell onto the Bankers Boxes. "You are having me followed?"

"Only because I knew I couldn't trust you once you got a taste of Christian." The voice at the end of the line was lined with fire.

Toni tipped back her head and stared at the ceiling. "This is not the first time I have done this. I have seduced many men before. Escorting them and sleeping with them is part of the plan. You taught me that."

"I did, but you're falling in love." The lingering silence seemed heavy. "What have I told you about love?"

"It leads to nothing but heartache," Toni answered and, for a long moment, said nothing else. "I don't want to do this anymore."

Her mother exhaled a long breath. "Baby, you think Christian, one of the richest bachelors in the country, is going to be interested in you, a penniless bastard girl who seduces men for her living."

Her mother's specialty was hurting and was succeeding. Toni wished she had a drink to wash the nasty feeling and awful taste her mother's words left in her.

"Christian is not like that," Toni murmured.

Christian made Toni feel loved and wanted. Christian was gentle and considerate when they made love. None of her past conquests fulfilled Toni or made her feel as loved as Christian did. Until Christian, Toni hadn't known what it felt like to be cuddled and held while watching the sunrise light the sky blue and bright from bed. Until Christian, no man made Toni feel wanted and special. Until Christian, the men in Toni's life only wanted physical satisfaction and, when they were done with her, tossed her away.

Christian didn't do that. Christian was a man of substance. Until Christian, the idea a man could care for her never entered Toni's mind.

"All men are like that. They're users and abusers. They're selfish children with no regard for anyone's feelings." Her mother asserted.

"Christian is not like that at all." Toni paused for a moment. She breathed heavily, then continued more firmly: "I don't want to do this anymore."

Her mother laughed raucously. "You're doing this, and you're finishing it. This is payday, baby. It's our survival. It's you and me against the world. It's always been just you and me, baby," her mother said more softly.

The guilt slivered through Toni—something else her mother was good at doing. But Toni loved her mother and understood the nature of her. She was her only family, and that carried a heavy emotional price tag that pressed down on Toni's chest.

Toni's fingers drummed on her thigh. "Vanessa Dobey," Toni said regrettably.

Chapter 22

IN BROWN LEGGINS and a white tank top, Toni sat on the stool at the kitchen island and watched Christian moving about his kitchen making dinner. Rigatoni alla vodka was on the menu tonight, and the sweet smell of the bubbling tomato sauce and sautéed garlic painted the kitchen. Between his cooking, sexual abilities, and handsome good looks, Christian was every woman's dream man. No woman would walk away from him, but Toni might—not by choice.

Her mother was right. Toni was falling in love or maybe falling in infatuation with Christian. Toni didn't know the difference. She had never been in love and didn't know what she felt.

Love was a commodity in Toni's life, fabricated to achieve the ultimate goal—the acquisition of money.

"You must never fall in love with a man. Love clouds your mind and deters you from what you must do. No man is to be trusted. All they do is fuck you up one way or another." Her mother's words rolled in Toni's head.

The repercussions of the one act perpetrated against her mother by the man, who might be her father, triggered resentful, hateful emotions that reverberated years later. It shaped her mother's life and, by association, Toni's. Either way, Toni had to compartmentalize her feelings for Christian to fulfil what she came to do. Besides, as Toni's mother was keen to point out, when Christian found out who she really was, he would want nothing to do with her.

How could Christian justify bringing a con artist, who gave her body for profit, into his perfect family circle? Toni was damaged goods and would forever be that way.

The humiliation on top of the hurt was more than Toni could stand. Toni's eyes blurred.

Turning away to avoid Christian's scrutiny and compose herself, Toni walked to the sliding doors. Outside, a spring rain fell, a steady drumming. The smell of wet grass and soil was strong. Looking past the rain, Toni thought she saw the reflection of—what?—a camera lens, a monocular.

The anger rose in Toni. Goddamn, her mother.

Instinctively, Toni closed the blinds to blind the intruder. "You do not mind if I close the blinds?"

Christian was adding the vodka sauce to the drained pasta. "You don't need to ask me. *La mia casa è la tua casa.* You're at home here."

How Toni wished she was. Toni's heart shattered into a million pieces.

"I got Bianca's approval of your project. Congratulations." Christian's curls flowed around his smiling face, and he wore jeans and white cotton.

Christian was in a rocking mood tonight, and Led Zeppelin's "Stairway To Heaven" flowed from the speakers.

"Thanks to you," Toni said.

"I was a small part of a big picture." Christian spooned sauce-covered pasta onto two dishes and grated parmesan over each. Walking the pasta dishes to the table, Christian stopped, looked at her in the eyes, and said,

"This was all you—your idea and contact. You. Come to the table. Dinner's on."

Toni took a mouthful of pasta and said, "My compliments to the chef."

Christian kept his eyes on Toni while he drank wine. "I like you being here."

"I like to be here with you."

"Then why not make it permanent."

Toni's eyes widened, and she set her fork down with a clatter. "What are you saying, Christian?"

"Move in with me," Christian said and watched Toni turn contemplative eyes toward the wine in her glass.

Toni was triumphant. She had accomplished the first step of her plan in record time with little effort. Her mother would be pleased to know that she had achieved the first two steps of her plan to make Christian fall in love with her and have him ask her to move into his home in record time. Toni would be thrilled with her competency if her achievement didn't rattle her to the core.

Toni looked at Christian demurely and said, "That is not a good idea, Christian. You barely know me." Toni's eyes remained focused on the red liquid in her glass.

"I know you and know you well. There are so many pluses to moving in with me. I have lots of room. If you like, you can set yourself up in one of the bedrooms, although I hope that won't happen. I want to slip into bed next to you at night and wake up looking into your eyes in the morning. I want you with me, Toni."

Toni saw the love for her reflected in his eyes. Toni's stomach churned. She drank.

"We can drive to work together, which is another plus. Using one car will reduce our carbon footprint. Kill two birds with one stone."

Looking more sullen, Toni took a longer sip of wine, aware Christian was looking at her directly.

"Are you hearing me, Toni? I want us to be together." Christian drew back in his chair and waited for her to speak. When she made no effort to do so, Christian said what he thought he'd never say to any woman, "I love you, Toni."

She averted her gaze when the pain stabbed her like a serrated knife to the heart. You felt hurt and pain, not when it was most likely but when it was most awful. Why did love have to be so complicated? Toni never thought she would hear those words, and now that such a lovely man said them from the heart, it broke her.

The silence between them lengthened. Led Zeppelin segued to a rebellious Pat Benatar who declared love was a battlefield.

"I never said those words to any woman before you." Christian's eyes didn't leave Toni's face.

The silence seemed heavy.

It was some time before Toni leaned forward slightly in her chair, looked Christian in the eyes, and said, "I told you, you must not fall in love with me."

"But I have," he said. "And I know you love me too."

Toni turned her eyes from him to the window. The blinds were drawn, but she knew what was beyond them. Toni thought of her mother. Toni thought of Christian. She thought of her empty life and the joy of family she would never have. Her thoughts went back and forth like a volleyed tennis ball. The volleying stopped when her thoughts went to her mother.

Toni felt immensely sad.

Turning her head, Toni looked at Christian. Lifting a hand to his face, she brushed her finger over his cheek. The feel of his beard against her fingertip felt good.

You must not feel emotion for Christian. Emotion will not play well toward the end goal, Toni told herself like a mantra.

"I love you too, Christian," she said, watching the thrill of the words dance through him and fill him with happiness. Christian felt as if he might explode. But it is not a good idea for me to move in. Not yet. I need some time to…. I just need some time." She avoided eye contact as she spoke.

Christian slid his fingers under her chin and turned her face until they were eye to eye. "I don't care about your past. Here and now is what I care about. I love you. You complete me, and I want you in my life."

Toni felt the pain fill her to the brim. Her stomach felt hollow. She had to do this.

Toni helplessly gazed at Christian. "All right, but you must keep the news of me moving in between us. For now." Toni was stacking the lies one on the other like a Jenga tower.

Christian watched her quietly for a moment. "I keep no secrets from my family. I told you they will not judge you, and they won't. It's not who they are."

But secrets were the essence of Toni's existence. "I am just not ready to face your family yet. It is too much too soon. Can you understand that?"

Christian's eyes stayed on her face. He saw shame, humiliation, and a lot of pain and thought that no one should have that in their life. Christian nodded his understanding, and in the quietest voice, he said, "I understand, and I won't say anything until you're ready."

Toni felt as if she died inside. "Thank you. I need a couple of months to give notice to my landlord, or I will lose my deposit."

"Don't worry about that. I'll take care of it."

Toni shook her head. "This, you and me, will not work like that. I take care of my stuff. Understand?" Toni drew out the word, and as quiet as her voice was, Christian heard her loud and clear.

Christian nodded and pressed a kiss to her lips. "Message received. I've grown up around I-take-care-of-my-stuff women and have the utmost respect for them and you. It's another reason why I love you." He was getting used to saying the words and liked their sound.

Toni didn't want respect, but she did need two months to do what she had to do.

Chapter 23

BIANCA TURNED HER attention from her laptop to Lorenzo when he walked into her home office. He wore jeans, an untucked rose-coloured polo shirt, and loafers. He carried their usual after-dinner drinks of Frangelico.

"The girls doing their homework?" Bianca took the glass Lorenzo offered.

Blooming light from the Murano lamps on the end table and desk cast light in the room, and Bianca's scent was everywhere. Behind the carved desk were bookcases with reference books, artifacts from Lorenzo and Bianca's travels, and family photographs. A large picture window gave a view of the side garden riotous with spring colour.

"They are. Serena was introduced to fractions today and is requesting help." Lorenzo eased a hip onto the corner of the desk.

"Shit." Isabella leaned back in her desk chair. She changed from her business-professional look to comfortable leggings and a black cinched pullover. Her hair feathered around her face, and aside from her wedding ring, she wore no jewelry. "You know my phobia of numbers. Unless analyzed, computed, and with a dollar sign in front of them, I'm not a fan of numbers. And, Christ, fractions are the devil's work."

"And I am a designer. I know colours, fabric, lines, and stitching, not numbers." Lorenzo took a sip of Frangelico and savoured the sweet, nutty taste on his tongue.

"Our daughter is doomed." Bianca gave her husband a brisk look. "I'll flip you for it. Rock, paper, scissors?"

A quirky smile played around Lorenzo's mouth. "Breathe easy. I told her I would go up in a while to help her."

"Thank you." Bianca looked up at her husband when the thought came to her. "You were playing me."

"I would never do that." Lorenzo leaned down and brushed his lips to hers when she started to speak, tasting the liqueur on her lips. "You are checking how your plan is working out?"

Bianca pointed to the blog on the laptop's screen. "It's working out better than I anticipated. The comment Toni talked Ming into posting to her blog has garnered over ten million views and almost as many comments in under one month."

"Wow," was all Lorenzo could say.

"Wow, is right. The power of the internet. And to think ten million views is minimal since Ming and her teammates have over seventy million followers combined. For my objective, they're already getting the necessary traction."

"The power of the internet indeed."

"Assuming some of the followers are bots, many are genuine comments. I don't know how to figure out exactly how many hits the comment has on Weibo, but in one month, it's generated more than enough attention." Bianca watched the smile flicker on Lorenzo's face. "What's that grin for?"

"You, *amore*. You sound like a full-fledged geek."

"I need to be acutely attuned to anything relating to my decisions. Don't I?" There was a doubtful inflection in her voice.

"If that is what you believe you must do, then yes. It is what makes you a great leader. There is no perfect playbook for leadership, but you are doing it right. I just never imagined my wife to be a computer geek."

Bianca gave him a huge smile. "I didn't either."

"Will they be able to track you when you visit these websites? They," Lorenzo air quoted the word, "should not."

Bianca nodded. "IT set me up with a VPN so that I'm untraceable. I need to follow the instructions I've committed to memory." Bianca pressed a finger to her temple. "Don't want to leave a trace. Don't ask me how that works. I may be a computer geek, but I am nowhere close to being as technically knowledgeable as our IT team—or Toni, for that matter. Sometimes, I think those kids speak in tongues."

Lorenzo walked to the sitting area and sat on the buttery soft leather sofa. "Your plan is working well, then."

"I have to admit it's worked like a charm. Even the one comment purposely posted by Ming to Toni's blog has weeded out fifteen more women claiming Bob sexually assaulted them. One of the women claims he fathered her child." Bianca sat next to Lorenzo when he waved her over.

"And how are you bringing these women's names to Marty's attention since you cannot be associated with any of this?" Casually, Lorenzo played with Bianca's hair.

"I didn't have to say anything. Marty's team came up with the idea of scouring the internet on their own. It turns out that when they typed Bob Klein's name, they came across Toni's blog, which now has over one-quarter million followers and as many posts after a few weeks.

Anyway, amid those posts, they uncovered comments from women who claimed to have been Bob's victims. Better than that, an unanticipated surprise I didn't expect arose when Ming got traction in Asia. As it turns out, Mr. Klein left his mark there, too. There are a handful of Asian women who have come out claiming they crossed Bob's path and were left wishing they hadn't."

"He was very busy. When did he have time to give to his family and work?" Lorenzo signalled for Bianca to set her feet on his lap.

Bianca toed her slippers off and set her feet on Lorenzo's lap. "Boggles the mind. He's such a meek-looking man."

"Maybe around you, he was meek. I mean, you are a formidable woman. No one is going to mess with you."

"Rub," she said, wiggling her toes. "Anyway, the Asian response will hopefully ensure that however Bob plans to sabotage the boutique launch, it will backfire on him."

"Proves what a formidable woman you are. You did all that without lifting a finger." Lorenzo ran his thumb across her sole.

"Well, I did get a few gray hairs along the way."

"I did not notice, but that is why God invented hair dye and hairdressers."

Bianca's brow cocking high, she took a swig of her Frangelico. "Rub," she said, offering her other foot.

"Is this not going to have an impact on the company? Bob was an agent of the Farfalla company in China."

Bianca's gaze cut straight to Lorenzo's face. "That cunning mind of yours is a very attractive feature, husband of mine."

"Does that mean I may get lucky tonight? I am starting to forget how great you look naked."

Bianca's amused smile widened. "Maybe."

"I will pretty myself up just in case."

Bianca broke into laughter. "To answer your question. We are not implicated. Mom offered Bob an incentive of a larger bonus if he worked on the Chinese project as a consultant to keep the Farfall-Mesi name concealed in the event things didn't work out. Meaning, Bob was not an employee of the company when he was in China. It was Mom's way of safeguarding the company from what she presumed was coming down the pike."

Admiration shone in Lorenzo's face. "I believe that is what you call checkmate."

Bianca nodded and went momentarily silent, her gaze focused on some distant point.

The grimness that settled on Bianca's face told Lorenzo her thoughts went to where they had been every day for the past weeks. "Honesty is the best policy. You must tell Christian the truth before he finds out on his own you have been using the woman he loves as a pawn. Blood will be shed between siblings. It will not be pretty."

Bianca glanced at her husband out of the corner of her eyes. "I'm not so worried about telling him I plotted to use Toni's blog to battle Bob. That is minor compared to telling him she's the internal leak."

"You have proof it is her."

Bianca shook her head. "But I'm ninety percent certain. We hadn't had any leaks until Toni came on. Until now, I had Marty put out crumbs not to weed out the leaker but to put out information to counter-strike any possible attacks from Bob. That being accomplished,

Marty put out the last crumb, which will prove who the actual leaker is. If it is Toni, it's going to kill Christian."

Lorenzo arched dark brows. "I see."

"I hate doing all this, but I must protect the company and the Asian boutique project. If I don't, I'll have failed, and I can't fail. I'll let too many people down, and I'm Isabella Farfalla's daughter." Bianca gave Lorenzo a fretful look.

Lorenzo set her feet down and slid close to his wife. Taking Bianca's face between his hands, he said, "You are Bianca Farfalla. You have nothing to prove to anyone but yourself, and you will because you are smart, wise, and a remarkable woman."

Was it any wonder she was crazy in love with this man? Lorenzo never failed to wash the bad away. And those dreamy, dark eyes didn't hurt. Bianca grabbed Lorenzo's shirt and pulled him close, covering his mouth with hers.

Her tongue found him and took in the sweet taste of Frangelico. The kiss went deep and became passionate, urgent. There was a quick dip in his belly, and a strong spear of lust shot through hers, making them burn with need and want.

In seconds, they were tearing at each other's clothes. Lorenzo's mouth was on Bianca's, swallowing her frantic gasps. Her taste exploded inside him, making him burn with desire. The thrill of driving himself inside her intensified, and he moved to shed his pants. She helped.

"Daddy. Daddy, when are you coming to help me with my math?" Serena cried out from the top of the stairs.

Lorenzo and Bianca froze and, looking each other in the eye, said, "Shit," simultaneously.

"We love them," Lorenzo reminded Bianca, lifting his pants.

"Yes. They are the product of our love," Bianca said, lowering her shirt and brushing her hair from her face.

"I am coming, baby. Wait in your room," Lorenzo called back, zipping his pants zipper. "We are picking this up in"—Lorenzo checked his watch—"forty-five minutes in our bedroom. I should be done by then."

"Yes, yes, we are." Bianca caught her breath as she slipped her slippers on. "I'll bring the wine."

Lorenzo walked to the door. "No wine. Just bring yourself." He paused at the door. "Bianca, you are a woman. Hear me roar." Lorenzo threw her a wink and closed the door behind him.

Was it any wonder Bianca was crazy in love with that man?

Chapter 24

AT THE TAP on Bianca's office door, she looked away from her laptop's screen to see Marty standing there. He looked stylish in a three-piece gray pinstripe suit. In his left hand, he carried a manila file folder. Outside Bianca's office, the sounds of lively chatter from her staff, fingers busily clacking on keyboards or answering ringing telephones, was a steady stream.

Bianca waved Marty in. He closed the door and walked into the office bright with spring sunshine.

Bianca wore a short-sleeve cream-fitted dress that gave her a sensual but authoritative look. At her neck, she wore a thick gold chain and matching earrings. Her hair flowed in waves down her back and shoulders, and her makeup was flawless.

"Is everything okay, Marty?" Bianca gestured him to a guest chair, noticing his anxious look.

Bianca's desktop was covered with reports, file folders, and legal briefs requiring her approval and signature. Two Mont Blanc pens lay scattered amongst the papers. A discarded coffee cup sat on a coaster at one desk corner.

Marty sat in front of Bianca's desk. "We received a request from Bob's lawyers…."

"It's now lawyers. Plural," Bianca interjected.

Marty drew a deep breath. "Yes. He now has a team from the prestigious firm of Steinman and Partners representing him."

Bianca's lips stretched out in a smile. "We must have hit a tender nerve."

Marty looked at Bianca intently. "We did, but it's nothing to smile at, Bianca. This is leading to a big fight. We should be looking at bringing in reinforcements."

Bianca leaned forward and set her arms on the edge of her desk. "Spare no expense. Bring in whomever it takes and do whatever is necessary, Marty. I want this bastard taken down."

Bianca's eyes were alive with resolve, and Marty saw so much of Isabella in her. Marty hoped Bianca was as sturdy as her mother and could handle what was coming because it wouldn't be easy.

"I was hoping you'd say that, and we're ready for the fight, but there's more," Marty said.

"There's always more." Bianca's eyes were calm and levelled on Marty's. She said, "Well, Marty, what is the more?"

"We received a request from Bob's lawyers to reveal all we have on Vanessa Dobey."

The words filled Bianca with genuine regret, followed by anger. "Christ." Bianca sunk back in her chair.

The tail end of Bianca's crumb trail worked. Vanessa Dobey was one of the five bogus names planted in the sham reports distributed to the employees suspected to be the leakers. Vanessa Dobey was the name assigned to Toni.

How would Bianca explain to Christian that the woman he fell in love with had sidled up to him for company information? How was Bianca to tell her brother that Toni had betrayed him, her, and the company purposely and systematically? Regardless, the news was going to break Christian. It would break Isabella when she found out Bianca came between Christian and the only woman who gave him the resolve to settle into family life.

Today was one of the few days that Bianca hated her job.

"You cannot go in there, sir. Sir, please stop." Toni chased after Bob, who threw Bianca's door open and charged into the office like a hunting lion attacking its prey.

Bob's face was blushed red. Bob wore a sports jacket over a white Italian silk shirt and tan, pleated gabardine pants.

"You fucking bitch. I will destroy you as you've set out to destroy me." Lava-hot fury poured out of Bob.

Bianca's spine stiffened at Bob's menacing tone, but she kept calm. Marty bolted to his feet and stood beside Bianca to shield her from Bob.

"I am sorry, Bianca. He charged past me, and I could not stop him. I will get security," Toni said.

"It's all right, Toni," Bianca observed Bob closely. "There's no need for that. Is there, Bob?"

Bob ignored the question. "You fucking bitch, you've set out to destroy my reputation." The anger oozed from his pores.

"You did that on your own, Bob." Marty tossed in defence. "And I'd ask you to take caution in your tone and use decorum in this office."

"Oh, look, the lapdog talks," Bob said with biting sarcasm.

"That's the best you can do, Bob?" Marty's unimpressed eyes stayed focused on Bob. He wouldn't fuel Bob's rage or resort to his level. They may have been equals at one time, but no longer so.

"Have a seat, Bob." Bianca's voice and smile were cordial, but Bob knew better than to take it at face value. Deep inside Bianca, there was a hardness Bob had seen first-hand.

"I don't want to fucking sit. I want to know who you're paying to spread lies about me all over the interwebs." Bob's eyes looked feral as he stepped closer to Bianca's desk.

Bob stopped in his tracks when Marty put one hand up, palm out, to signal him not to come any closer.

"I don't know what you're talking about, Bob." Bianca looked subtly at Toni, whose body rigidified when she realized the man standing before her was Bob Klein.

"Don't play the innocent with me. I know you know exactly what I'm talking about, and I know you did it," Bob barked with the anger surging through him.

"I have no idea what you're talking about, Bob, but do let Marty and I know where you're getting this information. It may be useful to us when going up against you," Bianca's calm composure rankled Bob.

"I'm not fucking letting you know anything. You're a shrewd woman who plays to win. Have your lapdog here figure it out."

"There's no flaw in that logic. Thank you, Bob. Marty, file a request to Bob's lawyers for the information as they've submitted one for Vanessa Dobey's." Bianca saw Toni's face tinged with panic. "I just hope your information is factual."

Marty's gaze was steady on Bianca for a long moment as he decoded her last comment. When Marty did, he raked his fingers through his hair. "Vanessa Dobey doesn't exist. Does she? You fucking made the name up."

Bianca and Marty's blank expression conveyed nothing, while Toni's face turned turbulent with emotions. Bianca saw fear, and then anger fill Toni's eyes. To Bianca's surprise, Toni's eyes waned from anger into a wounded look. Toni walked to the sofa and sat, head bowed.

Toni wore a black suit over a pink silk blouse. Her hair flowed in waves to her shoulders. Her face was expertly made up.

"Why make a name up?" Bob looked at Bianca with a steady gaze for a long moment. "Shit," Bob said when the puzzle pieces came together in his head. Bianca was trying to weed out who the person was who was feeding him the names.

As much as Marty detested Bianca for destroying him and his career, he couldn't help but admire her Machiavellian mind. Bianca was Isabella's daughter. She was astute and as cunning a businesswoman as Isabella.

"Goddamn it, Bianca, I was loyal to the company for thirty years. I'm the one who introduced the idea of entering the Chinese market to your mother. I was the one instrumental in making it possible. Me." Bob pressed a thumb to his chest as he pointed out his accomplishments.

"I don't deny it, just as you can't deny the fact you would have benefited greatly from your effort if you hadn't been such a gigantic asshole, Bob," Bianca answered with a grimace. "You stole so much from those women because of what in that tiny brain of yours," she aimed eyes at his crotch, "you believe is your privilege as a man. Well, Bob, luckily for the civilized world, male privilege is becoming an outdated concept. It's no longer a thing, but consequences for your entitled actions are. I'd like you to leave, Bob. You're not welcome here."

Bianca's mild tone was in direct contrast to the fierce sea-blue eyes she cast at Bob. Bianca picked up the telephone and dialled when Bob didn't budge. "Mr. Holton, please send your security officers to my office to escort Mr. Klein out of the building, and please ensure he's barred from entering this building and all Farfalla establishments worldwide."

Bob ran a hand through the mass of peppered hair as he paced the room. "All I want is my bonus, money that I earned, which I now need to pay the mounting legal bills I've incurred because of you." Bob's tone was one of defeat.

"And I would have gladly signed off on your five million dollar bonus, but your male privilege got in the way." Bianca waved the security guards in. "Make sure Mr. Klein leaves the building. Permanently."

Bianca and Marty watched Bob being escorted out of her office by a security guard on either side.

"You stay, Toni," Bianca said when Toni rose to her feet.

"Go on back to your desk, Toni. I need a few minutes with Bianca. Close the door behind you," Marty said, and Toni did as told.

"What are you doing, Marty? I need to speak to her about being the leak."

"She's not the leak, Bianca."

Bianca's brow furrowed, and confusion filled her eyes. "What are you talking about? We've proven it."

"I think it's best if I show you." Marty slid the USB stick he dug from his jacket pocket into the port of her laptop. Compressing his lips, Marty slipped into silence to gather the strength to face what came next.

Marty set the video to play.

The woman sitting at the bar stool facing the camera was a beautiful brunette with high cheekbones and red-painted lips. She reached for the glass of wine and brought it to her lips. Seductively, she sipped, watching the man sitting beside her over the rim of her glass. His back was to the camera, but Bianca could make out the dark wave of hair and the hand that came up to rest on the woman's thigh, exposed by the slit on the skirt that rode high. Smoothing his hand up along her thigh, he slipped it between her thighs.

Bianca stopped the video and flicked her eyes from the screen to Marty. "What does this have to do with anything, Marty?"

"Keep watching." Marty fast-forwarded the video for twenty seconds and raised the laptop's volume.

"The next name that came up was Vanessa Dobey," said the man in the video, who spelled the name out for the woman.

The audio was poor, filled with background bar noise.

The woman moved closer to kiss the man on the lips. "You're a love. That name will get me closer to a partnership at the firm. I'm very grateful, and I want to express my gratitude."

"I'm up for that." His hand rode higher up her thigh. "My wife's at work—as usual. We have two hours."

The woman's smile widened. "What are we waiting for, my Italian stallion? Go book us a room, baby."

The man swiftly rose from his seat, and as he turned, the camera got a clear shot of his face.

Bianca's breath caught in her throat.

Chapter 25

BIANCA'S EYES WIDENING in shock and disbelief at what she saw on the screen, she paused the video to examine the man's face more closely. Pressing play on the laptop, she watched. She rewound and played the video again several more times. The same image came at her each time, and Bianca's stomach lurched every time. It was him.

Disappointment crushed Bianca's chest and shut off her air. Bianca shoved off from behind her desk and stepped away. Her mind racing, Bianca walked toward the credenza, pulled the door open, and fished the whiskey bottle. She poured a tall drink and took it in one swallow to settle her nerves. Bianca poured a second taller drink, hoping to stop the image from continuing to assault her. It didn't.

Bianca took a moment to settle her nerves.

Finally finding her voice, Bianca said, "The man on that video is not Lorenzo." Although the denial was strong in Bianca's voice, she couldn't conceal its jarring effect on her.

"I've watched the video several times, and I'm afraid it's him, Bianca." Marty watched her toss the second drink back and wince. "I'm sorry."

"Lorenzo would never betray me. He wouldn't be disloyal to me with any woman, let alone share confidential company information." Bianca's eyes weren't angry or resentful. They were hurt.

Feeling her pain, seeing it in her eyes, Marty looked away when he said, "I'm so sorry I had to bring this to you, Bianca."

Bianca pinched the bridge of her nose between her thumb and forefinger. "I know my husband, Marty, and that's not him. That's not Lorenzo. Where did you get this?"

"It was delivered to the reception this morning addressed to you in a plain envelope with no return address or indication of who delivered it." Now, Marty walked to the credenza and poured himself a drink. "As with most such packages, security checked it, and afterward, it was passed to me."

"Because there was a note demanding money to conceal it." Bianca stood over her desk, eyeing the frozen image of Lorenzo on the laptop screen.

It couldn't be him, Bianca told herself.

"Yes. I found the note in the envelope with the USB stick." Marty tossed the drink back and refilled it.

Bianca didn't take her eyes off the screen. "What did it say?"

"They're demanding fifteen million dollars to be paid in cryptocurrency to a numbered account in the Caymans and a twenty percent share in the company or the video is released on social media, and I quote, 'your billion-dollar Asian project crashes and burns before it's launched.'"

"Not asking for much," Bianca said.

Marty nodded and drank.

"Bring it over here, Marty," Bianca said, tilting her chin to the whiskey bottle on the credenza. "And whose name do we sign over the twenty percent share of the company?"

"No name. The note says they will contact us with the details once they receive the money." Marty emptied the remaining whiskey in the bottle in Bianca's glass.

Tossing back part of her drink, Bianca rewound the video, pressing play and listening. Bianca heard and watched the man's hand rise higher on the woman's thigh. "My wife's at work—as usual. We have two hours."

Bianca drank. The stimulation of the alcohol wound through Bianca's system, and she was calmer now. "This could be a stunt from Bob or his lawyers or both. I wouldn't put it past him to do something like this."

"Maybe his previous firm because I know Steinman and Partners prides itself on its solid reputation and wouldn't resort to such an ordinary stunt."

Eyes glued to the screen, Bianca watched the playing video. "I know my husband, Marty. This isn't Lorenzo. He'd never betray my mother, Uncle Carlo, or me. I'll speak to him and find out what the hell this is."

"You do not need to do that," Toni said, and Bianca and Marty looked up to see Toni standing at the door. "I am sorry for intruding, but you did not answer my knock on your door."

"Toni, I told you I needed time with Bianca," Marty grumbled.

"It's all right, Marty. Come in, Toni." Bianca watched Toni, with head bowed, walk toward her desk. She remained standing. "What do you mean I don't need to do that?"

"You do not need to check with Lorenzo. It is not him." Toni's fingers drummed against her thighs.

"What are you saying, Toni? What do you know about this video?" Bianca's anxious voice shot a wave of guilt through Toni.

Bianca had enough to deal with in her everyday life without having the additional stress caused by her, Toni thought.

"I leaked Vanessa Dobey's name, not Lorenzo. He would never do such a thing to you." Toni stared at the floor.

"I know he wouldn't." Bianca stared intently at Toni. "Whom did you leak it to?"

"My mother," Toni murmured without looking up. "I gave all of the women's names to my mother."

Bianca sat, and like a protective father, Marty stood beside her, his hand resting on her shoulder.

Bianca's eyes levelled on Toni and said, "Why? For what purpose?"

Toni was motionless as her eyes filled. "No matter what I say, it cannot justify what I have done to you."

Bianca sat back against the high back of her leather chair. "No, you can't justify betraying me."

It was Toni who felt betrayed by her mother. Toni believed her when she said she was using the information to extort money, not to help a sexual predator. Bob Klein hurt her friends, the only ones Toni had, and her mother, as usual, sabotaged that which made her happy.

Because of her mother, Toni betrayed Bianca, the only person who allowed her the opportunity to prove herself and believed in her. She crossed her friends; worse, Toni betrayed Christian, the only man who told her he loved her and meant it.

What was Toni to tell Christian? How was Toni to explain to him what she had done? Nothing Toni could say would expunge her indefensible actions.

"Marty and I need to know what the leaked information will be used for." Bianca and Marty waited and watched Toni absently, anxiously playing fingers against her thigh.

"For money." Goddamn her callous, greedy mother. "It is always for money for Mama." Toni was on the verge of a flood of tears from bursting.

"Don't give us the teary-eyed look." Marty cut in sharply. Heat flashed in Marty's eyes. "Goddamn it, do you know the compromising position you've put us in?"

Toni had no answer.

"Marty, give me a minute with Toni." Bianca gave him the okay nod when Marty didn't move.

Bianca got an unopened bottle of cognac and a glass from the credenza and walked it to her desk. She refilled her glass with cognac and poured into the second one.

Bianca slid the glass across the desk to Toni. "Sit."

"Thank you." Toni drank deeply to wet her sandpaper-dry mouth.

For a long while, they drank in awkward silence.

"Do you think your mother passed all the information you gave her to Bob?" Bianca asked, breaking the unnerving silence.

"After what she went through, I never imagined she would pass it to Bob Klein." Goddamn, her mother.

"That's not what I asked, Toni," Bianca said calmly, but her anger became more difficult to control.

"If he is working on getting you to pay him five million dollars, she will have given it to him, for a price, to help him win his case and extort money from you. It is what Mama does."

Bianca was silent momentarily, considering whether to tell Toni about the extortion note, but thought better of it. "You think Bob paid her for the information," Bianca asked.

Biting on her lower lip, Toni's fingers played faster on her thigh.

"I need to know, Toni. It will be useful information for us to determine our next step."

Toni breathed in deeply and exhaled an elongated breath. "Mama can never have enough money. She does not do anything without expecting payment in return and will do anything necessary to get her hands on it. Anything. I mean, she has used me to do what she must. She resents you. She believes she is entitled to a piece of your company."

Sitting forward with a jolt, Bianca asked in a puzzled voice, "Why does she believe that?"

"You have too much money. It is not fair for one person to have so much." Toni lifted her shoulders and then let them fall. "It is the way she thinks. It is what she made me believe, and when Mama sets her mind on something, she will get it at any cost."

Bianca paused. Sitting back in her chair, she stared at the defeated woman before her. "I thought you liked working here, that we had mutual respect for one another, and that you wanted to help your friends."

"I do like working here. I love this job, and I have great respect for you, Bianca. I have learned much since I work for you. And I do want to help my friends." Toni's anger swelled, and she plunged to the depths of cynicism. She was determined to hurt her mother as much as she hurt her. "I will prove to you I mean what I say. I will deal with my mother. I will make her pay for all she has done to you and my friends." And to me. Toni's eyes were hard as stone.

Bianca caught a glance at her laptop screen. "Why do you say this isn't Lorenzo?"

"Mama is notorious for putting out deepfake videos," Toni explained when Bianca's eyes puzzled. "They are fake videos where you use the likeness of a person in place of another person. May I see the video?"

Bianca turned the laptop toward Toni and pressed play. She sipped at her drink, watching Toni study the video.

After the third viewing, a gleam filled Toni's eyes. "It is a deepfake. It is not very good, but good enough to say what they want to."

With a jolt of relief, Bianca sat up ramrod straight in her chair. "Are you sure?"

"Positive. Aside from the poor video quality, which I believe is done on purpose, listen to this." Toni rewound the video and pressed play. "Do you hear it?" Toni replayed it.

"I do now. Lorenzo never contracts his words. He'd never say I'm up for that or my wife's at work. He'd say I am, and my wife is," Bianca said, and Toni nodded. "But it sounds like him."

"That is why they are called deepfakes. The people in the video are made to look and sound like the real person. Faces or bodies are—how do you say?" Toni rubbed at her temple, hoping to raise the words to the surface. "Umm, digitally altered. "They are designed to look like someone else." Only a trained eye can break them down. You must give the video to the IT department to look at it and get an investigator to dig up the original video."

Christ, what a world we live in. "Do you know who the man speaking is?"

"It is a guess, but if I know Mama, the man in the video is Bob Klein."

Assuaged by what she heard, Bianca felt a weight lift from her shoulders. "Thank you, Toni. One more question. Who's your mother?"

Toni aimed her eyes out the floor-to-ceiling window, which offered an excellent view of the lake and park. People sat at benches, enjoying the view of the lake, which was as smooth as glass and reflected the rays of sunlight. Boats glided across the serene water, and geese and ducks winged under an endless, cloudless sky, honking and quacking. Everything and everyone went about their daily lives, enjoying the simple pleasure of it and making the most of it.

Toni suspected her mother had gone the deepfake route when she refused to pursue the marriage with Christian and secure the flow of money she demanded. Toni could only imagine what her mother threatened to do with the video, and she had to correct things.

"As much as I hate her right now for what she has done to me, you, and my friends, she is my mother," Toni said, surprised to see Bianca nod in understanding. "I will deal with her. That I promise you." Her blue eyes flashed defiance.

"You know I have to fire you."

Toni nodded, the movement of her head barely perceptible. "I am sorry, Bianca. I did not want to do this to you. You have been the best boss I have had. You are the only person who has believed in me and made me believe in myself." Tears were shimmering in Toni's eyes, burning them.

"You've been the best assistant I've had, Toni."

"Thank you. That means a lot coming from you."

"Christ, Toni, if you liked this job so much, why do this?"

"You don't say no to Mama." Eyes brimming with tears lifted to Bianca. "This will not affect Ming and the team, will it? Ming and the girls have done nothing."

"It will not. The Ming Project is a good, solid investment for the company."

Toni took the tissue Bianca handed her. "Thank you. They like Margie. Maybe she can take over for me."

"I'll give it some thought."

"Toni hesitated for a beat. "You will tell Christian everything," she said in a quavering voice.

Bianca shook her head. "You will."

"I cannot. I … cannot."

Bianca suddenly understood what Toni meant to do. "You can't leave without speaking to him, Toni. He's in love with you."

Toni got to her feet. "And I am in love with him. It did not start that way, and it was not what I meant to do, but I fell in love with him." Toni blinked back the tears. "It is the first time I am in love, and I do not want to hurt the only man who has ever loved me." Toni's voice was raw with guilt and regret.

"Christian will be devastated if you disappear without a word."

"He will not once he finds out what I have done. He will hate me," Toni replied and left.

Chapter 26

TONI'S SUDDEN DEPARTURE broke Christian's heart and him into pieces Bianca didn't think could be put back together. Bianca had never seen Christian react as he had for any woman. Until Toni, the women in Christian's life came and went without consequence. Toni had reached deep inside him. Christian was in love for the first time, and for the first time, he felt a hurt like he hadn't before.

After throwing Bianca out of his home, Christian refused to speak to her, Lorenzo, or anyone who came to Bianca's defence. Christian didn't eat or sleep, and for the first time in memory, he failed to show up for work.

Days that felt like an eternity turned into weeks for Christian.

Christian burst into Bianca's office. "Where is she, Bianca? Where's Toni?"

Startled, Bianca glanced up. "Jesus, Christian." She barely recognized her brother.

There were dark circles under Christian's eyes from lack of sleep. Christian's hair was messy, and his face had several days of growth and stubble. He wore gray sweatpants, a matching sweatshirt, and running shoes.

Christian looked like a lost and broken man. Bianca's heart hurt for him.

"Where's Toni?" Christian's pace accelerated, and so did his anger as he walked toward Bianca's desk. "I know you know where she is."

Bianca set the pen in her hand down. She wore a white A-line dress with a wide black belt. Her hair was tied into a twist. Although it was late in the day, her makeup was impeccable. "I'm sorry, Christian. I don't know."

Out the glass wall, rain drizzled from a dark sky, blurring the evening skyline. The smell of spring rain, wet earth, and damp grass permeated the air. Bianca's office was bright with white light from the ceiling pot lights.

"The hell you don't. You know everything," Christian barked.

"I don't. I've tried to track her down, but…." Bianca paused when Christian hit the desk with the palms of his hand and leaned in with a menacing expression.

"I know you know exactly where she is," Christian said, his voice rising, hardening.

Bianca overlooked the menacing tone. "I honestly don't, Christian." The hurt on his face made her want to reach out to pat his hand, but she refrained for fear of how he would react.

"This is all your fault. You were plotting to use Toni from the beginning. I didn't know what you planned to do, but I saw that conniving look in your eyes. Tell me I'm wrong." Christian stared at Bianca, his blue eyes blazing with pure anger.

"I wanted to use her blog to expose Bob Klein and nothing more. I never expected the outcome to turn out as it did. I never imagined she would leave and disappear. I'm sorry, Christian."

"Her name is Toni."

"Yes, of course. Everything I told you was the truth, Christian. I never meant to hurt you. I wanted Toni to tell you everything so you could forgive her as I knew you would have." The sincerity in Bianca's voice sliced at Christian's anger.

"I would have." Christian's fuzzy head bowed.

The silence was thunderous. It was seven p.m., and aside from a handful of workaholics still at their desks and the security guards making their rounds, the office was quiet.

"I am sorry," Lorenzo said when he walked into Bianca's office to tell her he was heading home and saw Christian sitting in the guest chair. Christian's elbows rested on his knees, and he covered his face with his hands. Lorenzo thought he heard Christian whimpering.

Reinforcements, Bianca thought and waved Lorenzo in. "Close the door behind you, honey," she said softly.

Lorenzo walked straight to the credenza and poured three glasses of whiskey neat. "Have this, Christian." Lorenzo wore a lime-green vest over a yellow buttoned-down shirt and black, pleated pants.

Christian didn't look up and said nothing. Lorenzo set the glasses on the desk and settled into the empty guest chair.

Bianca and Lorenzo drank in silence until Christian looked up. "Toni wouldn't leave without first talking to me."

Bianca took a moment to gather her nerves, and only when Lorenzo nodded, encouraging her to continue, did she say, "There's something I need to show you, Christian. It will explain why Toni left without speaking to you."

Bianca walked to the safe concealed behind Isabella's framed first pencilled design. She clicked it open and retrieved the USB stick.

"Watch this, Christian. Please, Christian, watch this," Bianca repeated when he refused to flick his eyes toward the laptop.

Not entirely convinced he wanted to see what Bianca had to show him, Christian slowly turned his eyes to the laptop's screen. Bianca pressed play, and the video flashed on the laptop's screen. A breathless hush filled the room as the minute-long video rolled on the screen.

Christian sat still, intently watching.

"That is not me," Lorenzo said defensively when the video ended.

"I knew it wasn't you the minute Marty and I watched the video," Bianca said.

A frown line deepened between Christian's eyebrows. "What is this? Why has Marty seen this? What does this have to do with Toni?"

"This USB stick was addressed to me with a ransom note for fifteen million dollars and some other nonsense. The mailroom gave it to security, who gave it to Marty when they found the ransom demand. Marty brought it to my attention," Bianca paused to breathe. "Toni admitted that her mother made the video."

"She's lying, right?" Christian looked from Lorenzo and back to Bianca when Lorenzo said nothing. "You're lying."

Bianca didn't defend herself but proceeded to tell Christian everything. "The video is what they call a deepfake. The best I can describe it is that they take your image and voice and paste them over the actors in the video."

"I know what a deepfake is." Christian, pale and drawn, rose to pace the room. "Everyone in the office knows about this video?"

Bianca shook her head. "I would never allow that. Only Marty, Lorenzo, Toni, and I saw the video. And now you."

Christian gaped at Bianca. "What are you saying?"

"We need more alcohol." Lorenzo walked to the credenza, picked up the bottle, and refilled everyone's glass.

"Toni admitted her mother is the woman in the video and believes the man with her is Bob Klein."

Confusion and despair bubbled into anger. "So what? You said it's a deepfake." Christian's voice was touched with acerbity.

"Toni told me…." Bianca wavered.

"Speak, Bianca. Let's hear how you'll cover your ass this time for whatever scheme it is that you orchestrated." Temper had whipped colour into Christian's scruffy face.

Sitting back in her chair behind the desk, Bianca took a moment before she said, "Toni said her mother does this often to extort money from men." Bianca reached for her glass and drank before she went on. "You heard the fake Lorenzo in the video mention Vanessa Dobey."

Christian rubbed at his temples to soothe the headache expanding inside his skull. "What of it?"

Bianca breathed in deeply. "Vanessa Dobey is a made-up name I came up with when we discovered an internal leaker was disclosing information about the Bob Klein lawsuit. In particular, the names of the women who suffered Bob's sexual abuse and whom we plan to use against Bob. I had Marty plant five fictitious reports, with a made-up name for each of the five people we presumed to be the leakers. Vanessa Dobey was the name assigned to Toni." Bianca paused when everything seemed to wash over Christian: disbelief, anger, shock, and disappointment at once.

"Vanessa Dobey was the only leaked name?" Christian asked, and Bianca nodded.

Christian fell into silence, and Bianca and Lorenzo slid into the silence with him.

Questions and so many thoughts floated in Christian's head. Toni wasn't who Bianca portrayed. She couldn't be. Christian refused to acknowledge the woman Bianca portrayed was Toni because Toni wouldn't blatantly and purposely betray him.

Doubt followed, and Christian wondered if all Toni's words and actions were calculated measures to use him to gain access to company information.

Did Toni lie when she said she wanted to be with him? The question that haunted Christian was if Toni meant it when she told him she loved him.

"I asked her to move in with me," Christian said after some time passed. "She told me she couldn't just yet."

"I'm sorry, Christian, I didn't know," Bianca said.

"I told her I loved her, and she told me she loved me," Christian said in a low voice. "But that was a lie, wasn't it?"

Bianca's chest tightened, and she hauled herself to her feet and rounded the desk. "She does love you, Christian. She told me so."

"It is the reason she left, Christian. She didn't want to hurt you." Lorenzo propped the discarded glass of whiskey in Christian's hand.

Christian took the drink in one swallow. The drink went down smoothly and soothed the knots in his stomach. Christian held the glass out for Lorenzo to refill.

"Lorenzo is right, Christian. If Toni didn't love you, she would have stayed," Bianca said.

"Why did you have to get her involved in all of this?" Christian's voice was unsteady and thick as if forced through a tight throat.

Bianca held the blue eyes, swimming with pain. "Christian, she leaked information for weeks before I caught her. I trusted her. I gave her unimpeded access to all the information from this office. She betrayed my trust as much as she did yours." Bianca adopted a gentler tone when she said, "She didn't leave you, Christian. She left the situation out of guilt and remorse. I'm just sorry you were hurt in the process," Bianca said gently.

"Yeah, me too." Christian rose and walked out.

Chapter 27

BIANCA'S HAIR WAS bound into a ponytail. She wore comfortable jeans, an oversized sweatshirt, U of T stitched on the front, and ballerina shoes as she paced her home office, telling herself she was a grown woman, not a child. She was a wife and mother. For Chrissake, she was the head of a major corporation. She was woman hear me roar. Women in her position didn't turn to their mothers the minute things went south.

After anxiously pacing her home office for another ten minutes debating the pros and cons, Bianca sat behind the desk and made the dreaded call.

"Hi, Mom. Did I wake you?" Bianca said when Isabella's woozy voice answered the telephone.

It was two in the morning Italian time. The panic that sets in when you receive a call in the middle of the night made Isabella sit up abruptly in bed. Her almond-shaped hazel eyes, flecked with specks of orange, went wide with concern. "Is everyone okay? Are the girls okay? Are you…."

"Everyone's fine, Mom." Bianca cut in to ease her mother's mind.

Isabella let out a breath of relief. "How are you, honey?"

"Did I wake you?"

Isabella thought it was a diversionary question to gather her nerves. "No, honey, you didn't. Your father and I were taking in the night view from the terrace,"

Isabella said to ease her daughter into telling her the reason for her call, but Bianca's roving mind didn't hear a word her mother said. "What's wrong, honey?"

"Everything's gone wrong, Mom. I screwed up big." I don't know how you did this job all these years, leaving with a sane mind and looking as good as you. I already feel like I've aged ten years and need therapy."

Isabella heard her daughter take a big swallow of what she imagined was a stiff drink. "Well, honey, I attribute my great looks to the skilled application of makeup and hair dye and my sane mind to alcohol. Lots of it."

Isabella brushed the chestnut hair from her face. She wore a colourful, floral patterned silk nightgown with white lace stitched at the low V neckline.

Bianca smiled. Trust her mother to come up with a witty response to make her feel better. "Do you have a minute, Mom? I need to talk to you."

"I have all the time in the world for you, honey." Isabella shushed Antonio, stirring next to her in bed. "It's Bianca. No, everything's all right. Go back to sleep. Yes, I'll tell her love and kisses from Daddy." Isabella slid out of bed and, closing the bedroom door behind her, walked to the tiled kitchen. The house was asleep, as was the outside world. Isabella flicked the ceiling light on. "What's wrong, Bianca?"

"Everything, Mom, everything is wrong." Bianca heard the pouring of water into a glass. "I don't think I can do this."

"You're my daughter. Of course, you can. Whatever is upsetting you is a bump on a long road teeming with many more bumps to follow. You must push forward because getting over that first bump is crucial to your confidence as an effective leader." Isabella slid a chair back from the thick oak table and sat. "Now, tell me everything."

ALL NIGHT CHRISTIAN CALLED TONI'S CELL phone. All of Christian's went straight to voicemail, and she didn't return any of his calls. Christian stopped calling and leaving messages when her voicemail was full.

Without Toni, the house felt empty, devoid of life. Christian could smell Toni's scent and hear her laughter. Christian imagined her sitting at the kitchen island, watching him make dinner as he made himself a sandwich that he had left uneaten.

Lying in bed, Christian absently reached for Toni in his sleep, but she wasn't there. In the darkness, his head pillowed on his hands, he lay awake for the rest of the night, staring at the ceiling.

Christian didn't know where Toni lived or spent her time. Aside from her mother, Christian didn't know if she had any family. Christian came to realize he knew nothing about Toni. How could Christian not know? He and Toni had spent months together, and he knew nothing about the woman he loved.

He intended to make Toni a part of his life forever, share his home, and raise a family. Now she was gone, his heart was broken, and he had no idea where to find her.

Christian rose from his bed and walked to the bathroom. Intently, he stared at his reflection in the mirror above the sink. Christian barely recognized the scruffy-looking, broken man he saw in the mirror. Christian didn't believe he could gather the pieces to move on with his life.

If this is how love felt, he wasn't falling in love again.

"CHRISTIAN'S HURTING, MOM, AND I CAUSED that pain. I hated myself for doing that to him, but I had to. I had no choice. I had no choice," Bianca repeated to justify her actions to herself.

"Honey, you'll be making many unfavourable decisions, which won't make you any friends. It's the nature of the job," Isabella said.

"He's my brother, and I manipulated the woman he's in love with for my means. I planned to use her to broadcast information to slander Bob's name and take him down for what he did. I couldn't let him get away, Mom. Not after what you went through."

Bianca didn't have to explain her actions to Isabella. She understood her daughter's motivation. "And your plan was brilliant, honey. Perfectly Machiavellian."

Bianca managed a brittle smile. "It was good, wasn't it?"

"I don't think I could have devised such a calculating plan. And to evolve into having her publish information on a Chinese social media forum aimed at getting the attention of the local government officials who approved our trademarks and permits to prevent Bob from sabotaging them was exceptional." Isabella thought she was past her prime the more they spoke about modern technology. "But the absolute brilliance of your plan to simultaneously gain sympathy and attention for our brand is…. Inspiring, yes, that's the word. I taught you well." There was a hint of pride in Isabella's voice.

"Jesus, Mom, admiration for the monster you created is not what I'm after. I hurt Christian." Bianca's tone was one of soft sympathy and guilt.

Isabella thought she taught Bianca well there, too. Nothing eased a mother's concern more than knowing her eldest daughter cared for her brother as profoundly as she did. "You didn't hurt your brother, honey. Toni did. She came into your life with a plan and set out to fulfil it. It's good you caught her when you did and fed her bogus information for weeks." Isabella's pride oozed in her voice.

"Focus, Mom," Bianca said. "I added to Christian's pain."

"I don't see how, honey. Toni was the one who toyed with his emotions. I'll talk to him."

"Would you, Mom? He'll listen to you. He won't even take my calls right now."

"Of course I will, honey," Isabella said, hearing the concern in Bianca's voice. "Now tell me about this Toni woman."

Bianca started by saying, "She was an excellent assistant. I hated to have to fire her." Bianca finished by telling Isabella everything she knew.

"Do you have a picture of Toni?"

"I just sent you one from when we attended the gala. I also sent you a copy of the Bob Klein video. What are you thinking, Mom." Bianca waited while Isabella fired up her laptop.

Isabella played the video. The shock flew into Isabella's eyes when she saw the video and Toni's photograph. "Jesus Christ!"

"What is it, Mom?" Bianca asked.

All Bianca heard in response was a louder and more shocked, "Jesus Christ!"

Chapter 28

BIANCA WALKED INTO Isabella's study while Lorenzo kept Consuelo, Isabella's housekeeper, occupied in the kitchen. Consuelo missed Isabella, Antonio's company, and Lorenzo's task to keep her talking while Bianca rummaged through Isabella's safe was easy for him. Lorenzo could talk your ear off if given the chance.

The room smelled of the lemon Pledge Consuelo used that morning to polish the wood to a shine. The blinds at the picture windows were drawn open to let sunshine pour bright. The walnut desk was darkly stained and polished to a gleam, while Isabella's favourite high-back leather chair was neatly pushed against it.

The cream-coloured leather sofa, matching chairs, and coffee table sat atop a thick rug. Framed prints of Isabella's gowns, worn by first ladies, celebrities, and famous supermodels, hung on the burgundy-painted walls. The south wall was covered by a bookcase with every design book imaginable and a big-screen television at the centre.

The drafting table Isabella had used throughout her career to design the thousands of garments that bore her brand stood by the tall window, where the light was optimal. Isabella was old school and refused to employ the modern gadgetry today's designers use.

Bianca rounded the desk and slid the wood panel to one side to reveal the safe built into the wall. Bianca keyed the code. At the click to indicate release, she took a long breath of air, held it, and let it out before she opened the safe's door.

Inside the safe were several pieces of jewellery and a stack of documents: Isabella's will, the house deed, company documents, and cash. Bianca sifted through the safe's contents until she found the blue felt box. Snapping it open, she lifted the satin cloth on which the pearls lay. As Isabella said, beneath it, Bianca saw the sealed envelope.

Bianca retrieved the envelope and sat on the chair. Her eyes stayed riveted on the explosive contents that had changed her life forever. Her tangled emotions triggered her mind to roll back eighteen years when Isabella revealed the dark secret she had carried for decades and raised the notion that Bianca might not be Antonio's daughter.

Bianca refused to accept anyone other than Antonio as her father, but the minutest of doubt remained ingrained in her mind. As the years passed, the thought waned, but now, she relived the moment again.

For good or bad, our lives are the consequence of our past, thought Bianca.

Glancing over her shoulder to ensure no prying eyes, Bianca tore open the sealed envelope. No one but her mother, and now her, knew of its existence. Bianca found the hair follicle her mother had kept in the sealed envelope hidden for decades. The memory rushed at Bianca in a massive flashback, and it all came back at once: Isabella's confession, Joe Smith's name, his actions against her mother, and his reappearance after years of absence.

Bianca hadn't imagined relieving the worst day of her life all these years later, and she didn't want to.

Why couldn't the past stay in the past?

Bianca rose to get herself a strong drink. Picking up the bottle, Bianca splashed Courvoisier XO into a glass and tossed it back.

Bianca's head whipped up at the opening door. Her face had such a stricken look that it hastened Lorenzo to say, "Are you all right, *amore*? I called for you, but you did not answer." It took a moment for Bianca to gather her composure and hand him the envelope. "What is this?"

"It's Joe Smith's hair follicle."

A look of shock filled Lorenzo's face. "Your mother had this in her safe all this time?"

Bianca nodded. "For security, and the time has come to use it."

"What are you talking about?"

Bianca told Lorenzo of her conversation with her mother and their plan to track Toni and end the Bob Klein lawsuit.

"*Gesù Cristo*! You Farfalla women are dangerous when you come together. I will sleep with one eye open from now on."

Bianca let out a half-smile and leaned in to brush her lips to Lorenzo's. "I can always count on you to put a smile on my face."

Lorenzo's eyebrows tilted. "I was not joking."

Bianca closed the safe door, turned the dial, and listened for the locking mechanism. "I'll do anything that will result in Bob getting his just desserts and donating his five million dollar bonus to the Farfalla foundation, then sign a cheque over to him." Bianca slid the wood panel close. "And make Christian smile again."

Lorenzo and Bianca sat side by side on the sofa. "What do you need me to do, *amore*?"

Bianca shook her head. "I can't get you involved. The next step of the plan requires doing things behind Christian's back. I don't want him to hate you as much as he hates me. You and Christian have a good relationship."

Lorenzo lifted a hand to her cheek. "I am your husband. You are my priority. Besides, I am a big boy and know how to handle the bromance between your brother and me."

"I don't know what I've done to deserve you."

"One, you are a tigress in bed. Aside from a good cook, it is all a man asks for, but you cannot have everything." Lorenzo's knee bumped companionably against Bianca's. "Consuelo said she wants to make us lunch. She says she misses not cooking her meals for anyone since your parents went on vacation."

Bianca refilled her glass and poured one for Lorenzo. "Okay, but we'll have to pick up the girls at Christian's place at one. They should be done with swimming by then."

"He said he will buy them pizza for lunch, and he does not want to see you, remember?"

"I'll use my presence as a distraction while you get something I need from his house."

Part III

The End

Everyone has a light in them. It's how you choose
to shine it that shows the world who you are.

—M.L. Lexi

Chapter 29

HISTORY HAD A way of repeating itself, Isabella thought as she sipped her tea.

Isabella was at this junction two decades ago and resigned to move on; she put the sordid experience behind her for what she thought was forever. Yet, here she was, visiting her feelings of violation, fear, and anger again. As subdued as the feelings now were, they were there.

Antonio supported every decision Isabella made throughout their married life and faced every challenge with her. Isabella kept no secrets from Antonio. In this instance, Isabella wasn't so sure Antonio would support her decision to reintroduce a past he didn't want to revisit. Isabella took the unprecedented step of opting for secrecy.

The shock of the planned reunion would be too much for Antonio, and Isabella didn't want to risk him talking her out of doing what she had to for their son's happiness. It was why Isabella planned tonight's reunion at Bianca's house and talked Antonio into rounding up Christian, Lorenzo, and their friends for a poker night at their home. The poker game would keep Antonio occupied while Bianca and Isabella put their plan in motion.

"She's half an hour late. Maybe she's not coming." Bianca glanced at her watch for the umpteenth time. She'd changed from her crisply tailored office suit to comfortable jeans and an olive-green shirt. Her hair was twisted into a single long braid.

"Please relax, honey," Isabella said, watching her daughter pace her study.

Beyond the window, stars glimmered in a black sky, and a round moon shone bright. The air was scented with the sweet smells of spring.

"This is a terrible idea. I should have never let you talk me into this, and I should have talked you down when you suggested we go through this scheme." Bianca walked to the console table behind the sofa. Picking up the Baccarat crystal decanter and two brandy snifters from the silver tray, she poured and gave one to Isabella. "Are you sure you're up to this?"

"I am, and I'm fine. The beauty of ageing is that past traumatic events become less significant as you endure a lifetime of experiences. And there is no shortage of them throughout your life. Sometimes, if you're lucky, you can even outlive your past. Persevering is the key to survival." Isabella sipped on her drink.

The chiming bell of the front door had both women locking eyes on one another. "Are you ready for this, Mom?"

"As ready as you are. Try to remember this is not for our benefit. It's for your brother." Isabella reminded her daughter. "Let's get this done."

Bianca looked up to see her housekeeper escort Toni into the study. "Thank you, Marisol. Please make sure we're not disturbed." When Marisol closed the door to the study, Bianca said, "Thank you for coming, Toni. This is…."

"Your mother," Toni said reverently, her eyes fixed on Isabella.

Isabella was the essence of style and class in an apricot sweater dress with a flared skirt and pearls at her neck. Meeting Christian's mother, the founder of the company Toni stole secrets from, wasn't what she expected or wanted to do. Toni shrunk on herself.

If Isabella sensed Toni's uneasiness, she didn't show it as she stood and put out her hand. "It's nice to meet you, Toni."

Toni hesitantly met Isabella's hand. "Bianca did not say you would be here. It is a pleasure to meet you, Mrs. Farfalla. I sense this is not a pleasure meeting."

Toni wore a white jacket with black lapels and buttons over a white lace blouse and ankle-high pants. Her blonde hair rained around her pretty face down to her shoulders. Toni's lips were painted red, and her eyes dusted bronze.

"I'm sorry for the ambush, Toni." Isabella's hazel eyes remained riveted on Toni. Meeting face-to-face confirmed Isabella's suspicions. There was no doubt Toni was Michaela's daughter. Isabella gestured to Toni to sit on the chair across the sofa.

"Can I get you a drink, Toni?" Bianca offered.

"Yes. Yes, please, something strong," Toni said, and Bianca poured a glass of brandy and handed it to Toni. Toni drank deeply and held it out for a refill. "I was surprised to hear from you, Bianca."

Isabella crossed one slender leg over the other with such grace Toni thought she made the ordinary movement appear extraordinary. "I'll have to admit that's my doing. Please sit, Toni."

Toni's eyebrows lifted in concern as she sat. "Yours? Why?"

"Mom believes she knows your mother. Intimately."

"I do not see how. We have lived on separate continents, and Mama has never mentioned you." If her mother were connected to people of this calibre and wealth, she would have crowed about it nonstop. Being a part of such esteemed circles was her mother's life ambition.

Isabella looked into Toni's blue eyes and slowly shook her head. "No, she wouldn't."

"I do not understand why you think you know her." Toni could feel the prickle of anxiety in her gut as she sensed the conversation was heading nowhere good.

"Your mother's name is Michaela Farfalla."

The statement genuinely took Toni aback. "She is not a Farfalla. If she were, she would have shouted that from the rooftop."

"But her name is Michaela," Bianca said.

There was a pause before Toni said, "Yes. Her name is Michaela, but our surname is Trevi."

Isabella reached for the photographs on the coffee table and turned them over to Toni. "That's your mother when we were children. That's her and me on Halloween, at our first communion, our christening, and in high school." Toni's flummoxed eyes remained riveted on the photos as she flipped through them. "Those are your grandparents, Gianni and Nina Farfalla."

Isabella and Bianca watched the tangles of emotions cross Toni's face as she ran her fingers over the photo of her grandparents. "I did not get to meet them. They died before I am born."

Filled with disbelief, Bianca said, "I can assure you that your grandparents were alive and well until ten years ago."

Ashen-faced, Toni stared at Bianca and Isabella. "What are you saying?"

"Gianni died of lung cancer, and Nina had a heart attack shortly after. Not before you were born, but ten years ago. I'm sorry, Toni," Isabella said in a motherly tone.

"I do not believe it. That is not what Mama told me." Toni's voice turned into a whisper, and her fingers tapped on her thigh to deal with the rinsing anxiety setting in.

Bianca picked up Toni's discarded glass and handed it to her. "Drink some. We can show you their graves. They're buried not far from here."

Dumbfounded, Toni drank. Three sips later, she felt calmer. "Why do you say my mother is a Farfalla? She would have bragged to anyone who would listen if she was."

Hazel eyes on anxious blue eyes, Isabella said, "There are reasons why she doesn't," and stopped there.

"If you'd like to know the reasons, Toni, Mom can elaborate, but understand that the truth sometimes is a terrible thing."

Toni let out a long, despairing sigh, knowing Bianca was right. But how could it get worse than concealing the existence of her grandparents or the fact that her mother was a Farfalla?

"It's just the two of us, and we take care of one another," her mother had said often enough that it became their mantra. But it was a lie. Toni wondered how many more lies there were. She silently evaluated the sad state of her life.

After some reflection, Toni looked at Bianca and Isabella. "Why do you want to tell me now? Is this your way to get back at me for what I have done to you? If it is, I want you to know I have made up for it. Some. In the past few weeks, my blog has brought out additional women you can use in your lawsuit against Bob Klein. Also, the Bob Klein comments have blown up in China and brought out more women there. Ming has told me that government officials have threatened to arrest him if he enters China. Bob Klein has become *persona non grata*."

"That's good and well, but my and my mother's reason for this meeting is for Christian."

"My son has been heartbroken since you disappeared, Toni." Isabella watched the guilt slide across Toni's face.

"He will get over it soon. Christian is a man with many friends." Toni's fingers tapped faster against her leg.

"Before you, my son never asked any ... friends to move in with him or told them he loved them. He was serious about you, Toni, and is heartbroken and devastated."

Toni's heart sank in her chest. "I told Christian he must not fall in love with me. I told him this many times," she whispered, her head bowed.

"You didn't tell him you were using him to get access to our company information." Bianca's tone was harder than Isabella thought Toni deserved. Toni was a victim.

Isabella said, "Forgive Bianca. She's still working through her anger."

"I do not blame Bianca for being angry with me. I did not want to do it, and I certainly did not want to hurt Christian. You must believe me," Toni said when she saw the dubious expression on Bianca's face. "I will admit that in the beginning, I set out to use both of you. But as I got to know you and Christian...." Toni looked at Bianca. "You believed in me. You let me lead the Ming project. No one has trusted me with anything before, let alone a multi-million dollar project. As for Christian, I never imagined I would fall in.... I did not mean to hurt him." Toni murmured.

"Your mother asked you to do it?" It was more of a statement than a question from Isabella.

Toni gave Isabella a silent nod.

Bianca curbed the impulse to lash out at Toni. "To what end?" Bianca said in a controlled voice.

Toni blinked back, the tears threatening to flow, and told Isabella and Bianca everything. "She wanted me to marry Christian to guarantee her a steady income." Now, Toni's mind raced as the thought surfaced in her head. "How is Mama related to you?"

"We're cousins," Isabella said.

Toni's jaw dropped when she put it together. Eyes widening, Toni dragged a hand through her hair in a gesture of absolute shock. "That makes Christian and me…."

"You didn't let me finish." Isabella cut in but, too consumed in her shock, Toni didn't hear her.

"*Gesù Cristo*!" Toni raked her hands through her golden hair. "I did not know. I did not know. She knew we were related, and she still made me…. *Gesù Cristo*!" Shamed-faced, Toni covered her face with her hands and rocked back and forth in her seat.

Isabella rose, crossed to Toni, and sat beside her on the sofa. "Michaela and I aren't blood cousins, and neither are you and Christian."

Toni's face clouded. "What are you saying, Mrs. Farfalla?"

"Call me Isabella. Are you sure you want to hear the truth, Toni?"

"I do not, but I must." Toni acknowledged with regret.

"Michaela's mother, your grandmother, had an affair and got pregnant with your mother. I didn't find this out until much later from my mother. Your grandmother,

Nina, for obvious reasons, kept the affair and your mother's origins concealed. Your grandfather raised Michaela as his own. He went to his grave believing she was his daughter."

Toni levelled incredulous eyes at Isabella. "Mama knows?"

Isabella shrugged her shoulders. "Your mother and grandmother were very close. My guess is she knows, and both kept the truth from Gianni."

Toni closed her eyes and rested her head against the back of the sofa. "I do not know who she is. I always thought we were close. It has been only the two of us, and I have trusted her. I had no reason not to." Toni looked Isabella in the eye. "Why would she not tell me any of this? Why would she not tell me she was a Farfalla?"

"Everything will become clear soon enough," Isabella said.

Bianca's desk phone rang, and she answered it. After a brief conversation, Bianca looked at Isabella. "Your driver is on his way from the airport."

Toni sat up straighter in her seat. "Mama is coming? You are bringing Mama here." Feeling the surging hatred for her mother rising in her, pressing on her chest, Toni bolted to her feet to leave. "I do not want to see her."

Isabella's hand clamped down on Toni's arm. "No, honey, it's not your mother who's coming. I would never let that woman into my children's home or mine." Isabella handed Toni the last photograph and pointed to the man standing beside Michaela.

Toni's eyes widened, and her knees went weak. She fell back on the sofa.

Chapter 30

HOLDING THE PHOTOGRAPH with both hands, Toni couldn't take her eyes off it. Staring at it dumbfounded, she saw her mother, young and beautiful in a stunning white gown, standing next to the man with dark eyes and chiselled good looks. Both looked so young and so perfect together.

Stunned, dazed, and confused, Toni stared at the photograph for a long while. Feeling suddenly overwhelmed, Toni propelled herself off the sofa to her feet and paced the room with nervous energy. In silence, Isabella and Bianca watched Toni mumbling to herself as she carved a path on the wood floor.

"Mama married?" Toni's voice trembled before she steadied it.

Isabella nodded. "Sit down, Toni."

Toni swung her head and stared at Isabella. "I cannot. I am too angry, disappointed, hurt and … and…." Toni rubbed at her temple where the headache formed and promised to become a full-blown migraine.

"The man in the photo, his name is Joe Smith," Isabella said.

Toni looked at the photograph again. "Mama never mentioned she was married. What else has she lied about?" Toni cast angry eyes on Isabella.

"Christian told me you don't know who your father is," Isabella said.

"Mama said she did not know who my father was." Toni felt her knees buckle when she pieced it together, and she fell back onto the sofa. "Are you saying this man is my father?"

"Mom is not just saying it. We know he's your father. I ran a DNA test, and as Mom suspected, it matched yours," Bianca said.

For a moment, Toni thought she had misheard. "DNA? How? *Gesù*, what are you saying?"

"The man in the photograph is your father, Toni. He and your mother were married in their early twenties. He left her after several years of marriage," Isabella told her.

Toni looked pointedly at Isabella. "Left her and me. That is why she has denied knowing him. She wanted to protect me."

"No, Toni, you've got it all wrong." Isabella talked, and Toni listened. "Your father had to leave her to save himself. Joe was an alcoholic, and your mother fed his addiction to get what she wanted from him. I'm going to leave it up to him to tell you everything. It's his story to tell. He's lived in Milan all this time, Toni. He owns a very successful construction company there. He didn't know of your existence. Had he known, he would have come for you. He has a family. You have two brothers and a sister."

The disbelief of what she heard and the shock coursing through Toni prevented the tears from flowing. The silence that followed felt heavy and endless.

Toni looked broken and lost, Isabella thought, watching as the tears finally spilled from her eyes. Michaela did that to her daughter.

Isabella's eyes turned tender. "Your father's eager to meet you, Toni. He's going to be here shortly?"

The tears stopped coming when the nausea rose fast and sharp in Toni. "No, I cannot do that. It is too much to process."

Isabella patted Toni's shoulder with assurance. "You can, Toni. He hopped on a plane and crossed an ocean the minute I called him and told him about you."

With a fuzzy head and eyes wet with tears, Toni looked at Isabella. "He did?" Toni's voice was that of a child, not a woman who had seen and experienced more than anyone should at her age.

"Yes, he did." Isabella brushed back the hair that curtained Toni's face. "Now, let Bianca help you clean up so you're presentable. We don't want to scare Joe away."

Toni gave Isabella a teary smile. "Do you think he'll like me?"

Isabella heard that naïve child's voice again. "He hopped on the first flight out after our conversation. What does that tell you? Now, go pretty yourself up. He's going to be here any minute."

Twenty minutes later, the study door opened, and Joe walked in. He looked stylish in the Italian-cut charcoal gray suit, white silk shirt, and gray tie. His face was tanned to a healthy bronze, and his thick hair dashingly grayed at the temples, was neatly combed back. Finely etched lines were around the eyes behind the square, black-rimmed glasses. He looked handsome and exuded an aura of success and distinction.

"Hello, Isabella." Joe put out his hand, and she pumped it. The last time they shook hands, Joe thought he would never do so again. The last time they met, Joe apologized for putting her through the distress and suffering he had. The last time they spoke, Joe told Isabella he loved her and had since high school.

Isabella had told Antonio everything Joe had said to her when he appeared from nowhere at the quiet, out-of-the-way café where she spent most mornings gathering her thoughts. Isabella told Antonio that Joe was there not to hurt her but to apologize for what he had done to her and put her through. Isabella reiterated to Antonio everything but that Joe told her he loved her because it served no one's purpose—least of all, Antonio.

Now, decades later, here Joe and Isabella were.

"Hello, Joe," Isabella said.

"It's nice to see you, Isabella." After all these years, she looked as beautiful as he remembered. "Time has been kind to you in all respects."

"It has been kind to you as well." Isabella pulled the hand Joe held tightly away. "Did you have a good flight?"

"How could I not, on the Farfalla private jet? Thank you for making it available to me." Joe's English lilt leaned some toward an Italian accent now. Isabella supposed that was a regular part of evolution when you spent much of your life living in a foreign country.

"My pleasure. Please, have a seat." Isabella gestured him to the sofa.

Joe sat. "I never thought we'd run into one another again, let alone get a call from you out of the blue. When my assistant told me it was you on the telephone, I was in disbelief and thought it a bad joke."

"Well, situations arise in our lives that tend to make strange allies," Isabella said, faintly smiling.

"Indeed they do." Joe scanned the many framed family photographs throughout the room of Bianca and her family, Christian and his mother, Maria and Sal. The photo of Isabella and Antonio struck a nerve. As much as Joe resigned himself to believing the better man had won

Isabella's affections, it still stung. "You have a beautiful-looking family, Isabella."

"Thank you. They keep me on my toes. May I get you a drink?"

"Yes, please. Whatever you're drinking is fine. I need something to settle my jittery stomach. I've been somewhat anxious since our conversation." Joe admitted taking the brandy snifter Isabella offered.

"I can only imagine the emotions that struck when you discovered the existence of a grown daughter you knew nothing about." Isabella took a seat in the chair across from Joe.

"To say I was shocked is an understatement, but I look forward to meeting her. Is she here now, Isabella?" Joe's eyes radiated the excitement and eagerness Isabella was delighted to see—precisely what Toni needed.

"Yes, she's freshening up." Isabella brought her drink to her lips and took a sip.

Seeing the thoughtful, narrow-eyed look in Isabella's eyes, Joe sat forward with a jerk. "What is it, Isabella?"

"I know little about Toni, and what I know came from my son."

"Christian, right? He's the reason we're here." Joe sat back and crossed his legs.

Isabella put down her glass and rose to walk to the window. The sky was alive with twinkling stars and a full, glowing moon. Over the darkened land, Isabella could see, under the hazy beams of moonlight, the shapes and shadows of the night. The freshly mowed stretch of lawn in the front yard was a smooth, green blanket.

"Yes, he's in love with her, but that's a discussion for a later time." Isabella turned to face Joe. "As I was saying, I don't know much about Toni, but I sense there's a lot to unpack. She seems broken and diminished, Joe, and now she feels betrayed by Michaela and you."

Isabella watched Joe knock the brandy in his glass in a single pull and set the glass down on the arm of the sofa. Anxiously and for a long, silent moment, Joe tapped his ringed finger against its side. The house was infinitely silent, and the tapping of Joe's gold ring on crystal and his heavy breathing were the only sounds in the room.

Isabella refilled Joe's glass. "I'm sorry, Joe. I say it not to upset you but to let you know you have much to deal with."

"I suspected as much. Michaela has a talent for breaking the human soul," Joe said when he regained his composure.

Knowing first-hand what he spoke about, Isabella nodded. "I believe she's happy to know she has brothers and a sister, a family, you."

"I hope so. It won't be easy for any of us. My wife and children have been supportive and receptive about Toni being my daughter."

"That's a start." Isabella settled back in the chair.

"The children and my wife are eager to meet her. But my wife has some reservations about bringing Toni into our family too soon, and I worry about that, too." Goddamn Michaela.

"With good reason. Toni's gone through more than young women her age should." Isabella paused and brought her eyes to meet Joe's. She could see the genuine concern in Joe's eyes. "But I think with family support and lots of love, Toni will be fine."

Joe looked at Isabella. As wise as she was beautiful, he thought. "Yes, I believe so too."

Isabella's gaze lingered on Joe. "I'm sure your family will give her both."

"Before I boarded the flight, my wife told me not to worry too much that we'll muddle through as we have everything else."

"She sounds like a smart and wonderful woman, Joe."

"She is. She was my salvation then and still is today." Joe sipped at his brandy. From above the rim of his glass, his eyes lingered on Isabella for a moment before he said, "Is Bianca my daughter also?"

Chapter 31

THE DOOR TO the study opened, and Joe swung his head to see Toni pause dramatically when she saw him. Seemingly uncertain, Toni hesitated and remained arched in the doorway. She couldn't keep her racing heartbeat regular if she forced it.

From beneath freshly mascaraed lashes, Toni stared at Joe. He was tall and handsome, well dressed and projected wealth and breeding. Joe was just the type of man her mother would be entranced with. But Joe had a kind face, unlike the men her mother drew into her lair.

Joe gaped. The picture Isabella sent him after they spoke on the telephone didn't do Toni justice. She was more beautiful in person.

Joe looked at the large, blue eyes nervously gaping at him. Joe saw so much of Michaela in the line of her face, her cheekbones, nose, the width of her mouth, the fullness of her lower lip, and glossy blonde hair. But he also saw so much of himself in Toni. Toni was his daughter.

Yet something else the bitch stole from him.

It had been a long time since Joe last saw or spoke to his ex-wife, Michaela, but she was still affecting his life in the worst possible way. How could Michaela have kept the existence of a daughter from him all these years? She told him she couldn't have children—childhood polio, she'd said—and he accepted it and settled for a childless existence. A daughter would have made a world of difference in his life. Toni would have been the positive in a vortex of unhappiness and misery dragging Joe into darkness.

"Toni, I'd like you to meet Joe Smith," Isabella said when the silence hung too long. "Your father, Toni."

The quick tremble that shattered through Toni when she heard "your father," the words she thought she would never hear, made her skin tingle and her heart miss a beat.

Speechless, Toni gaped at Joe. A sudden and intense sensation of connection assaulted her. The undeniable chemistry between Joe and Toni was palpable, and goosebumps rose all over her arms.

More silence and awkward staring between Toni and Joe persisted.

In the woman standing before him, Joe saw the soft, girlish sea-blue eyes that held the kind of wholesome dreams he wished his daughter to have. In Toni's eyes, he also saw broken and corrupted innocence by a lifetime of regrettable actions brought on by Michaela's demands. His hand tightened into a tight fist at his side. Had he been a part of Toni's life, he could have saved her from Michaela and herself.

"Have a seat, Toni." Isabella walked to Toni and escorted her to the chair when her body English telegraphed she was incapable of moving. "Can I get you a drink?"

Toni aimed nervous eyes away from Joe and toward Isabella. "Yes, please."

The outdoor lights cast cones of light over the gardens, plentiful with white, red, and yellow tulips, purple asters, daffodils, hyacinths, and lilies. The pool came into view to the left of the gardens, its underwater floodlights lighting it sea-blue. Inside the study, bright with light, the scent from the garden and the pool's chlorinated water wafted with the night's spring breeze from the opened window.

Isabella poured everyone a fresh drink and served it. In silence, they drank while Joe gave Toni a moment to catch her breath. Isabella watched Toni's nervous piano-playing fingers drum against her thigh while Joe tapped his fingers against the side of his glass in a similar motion.

"You look different than I imagined," Toni's voice finally cut the silence.

"*È buono o male*?" Joe asked in the language they shared.

"It is neither good nor bad." Toni threw him a sharper look. "You speak Italian."

"I mentioned to you that Joe lives in Milan. He's lived there for decades and is fluent in Italian," Isabella said.

"That's right." Joe wanted to reach out and touch Toni, just his fingertips on her face, a touch of the hand. She wasn't ready yet. "You're more beautiful than the photograph Isabella sent me."

Toni's shoulders lifted and dropped. "Thank you."

"I'm so very happy to meet you, Toni. May I call you Toni?" Joe said, smiling warmly.

Toni nodded. "My Christian name is Antonia, Antonia Trevi."

Joe's earlier warmth rapidly evaporated, and he shook his head. "Christ," he said under his breath.

Understandably, Isabella watched Joe bring the glass to his lips and take a healthy sip of his brandy. To have his daughter named after Isabella's husband, the man Michaela was in love with and who'd won Isabella over, was a tough pill to swallow.

Toni's brow furrowed, and confusion filled her eyes. "I am sorry. Did I say something wrong?"

Isabella rested her hand on Toni's. "No, you didn't, honey. It's just an emotional moment for everyone. Let's all take a breath. Joe, show Toni the photos of your family," Isabella said, venturing to guess Joe carried several in his wallet.

Joe's vanished smile re-emerged. "Yes, I came prepared just in case you were interested in seeing who your brothers and sister are. Would you like to see them, Toni?"

Toni gave a subtle nod, and Joe's eyes crinkled with a smile. Reaching inside his jacket pocket, Joe retrieved the thick wallet. Unfolding the accordion insert, he unfurled it to display a dozen photos of his family.

"This is Aurora, my daughter. She's twenty-seven. She's an architect married to Riccardo, who is also an architect. The girl standing between them is their daughter, my granddaughter, and your niece, Emilia. She's three years old." The happiness flowing from Joe's eyes made the room brighter.

"These are my two boys, Massimo and Matteo, thirty and thirty-one. Massimo is an accountant, and Matteo is a surveyor. The woman next to Matteo is his wife Mia, and their two boys, your nephews, Toni. Massimo is the playboy of the family. He's yet to settle down and hopefully will soon." Joe watched Toni closely look over the photographs. He thought he saw tears begin to form in her eyes, but she blinked them back. "This is my wife, Francesca. We've been married thirty-two years."

Toni saw the love radiating in Joe's eyes as he worshipfully eyed the photograph. Anyone who'd been married that long and still looked at his wife the way he did was a man of substance, Toni thought. Toni understood now why his marriage to her mother didn't last.

Michaela wasn't interested in a routine life, continuity, or stability. Michaela's interest was excitement and unpredictability, male variety, and money. And Michaela tried to instill the same in her, but Christian changed that. Christian showed Toni she wanted the love of one man, the stability of a meaningful relationship, and a loving home.

Resentment for her mother tightened Toni's belly.

"You have a beautiful family," Toni said.

"They're your family, Toni. They made the trip with me."

Toni was struck by panic and fear. Her jaw slackened as she stared at Joe. "Are they here?"

Detecting the tenseness in her voice, Joe said reassuringly, "Don't worry. They're not here. They're at the house we're staying at downtown." Toni's relief was immediate. "They're eager to meet you, Toni."

"Oh, I…. No. I do not know if I can do that." Toni's voice sounded tight as if her throat were closing.

"Sure you can, honey. This is your family now," Isabella said. "And as Joe said, eager to get to know you."

Toni stared down at the clenched hands on her lap. "They are successful, educated professionals with stable families and lives." Toni looked at the photos again. "They are so perfect. I am not that. I am not any of those things."

Joe thought there was something so sad resonating in Toni's eyes. Swiftly, like a tsunami riding to shore, the memories assailed Joe. He remembered Michaela berating, patronizing, denigrating, and beating every ounce of confidence and dignity from him. Joe sensed that Michaela had done as much to Toni. Joe could hear it in her voice, see it in her despairing eyes and her slumped shoulders.

Joe dreaded thinking about what Michaela had Toni doing for her.

Instinctively, Joe felt the need to smooth away the hurt he saw in his daughter's eyes. "I don't want to hear you say or believe such nonsense. You're your own person, your own woman with your own strengths, and as my daughter, you carry the intelligence gene."

"And the modest one," Isabella joked to add levity to a conversation that was becoming overwrought.

Joe quirked his brow. "I speak the truth. Weren't you managing a twelve-million-dollar program for Bianca?" Toni gave Joe a silent nod. "That says it all. Farfalla women don't entrust just anyone with such a responsibility."

Smiling, Isabella piped in and said, "Damn straight, we don't."

Joe smiled to himself at Isabella's resolute tone. "I won't push you to meet the family, Toni, your family now if you don't feel ready to do so. When you're ready, they'll be there."

There was no demand or pressure from Joe. Toni only heard the placating voice of a parent to comfort and soothe his anxious child. Feeling awash in what Toni now understood to be the genuine affection of a caring parent, her fears and anxiety washed away.

"If they are ready to meet me, then I am ready to meet them," Toni said with regained self-confidence.

"Meet who?" Bianca walked into the room, and Joe rose to his feet.

"Toni's extended family. This is my daughter, Bianca. Bianca, this is Joe Smith."

Bianca hesitantly and slowly met the hand Joe offered. The gamut of emotions overtook both Bianca and Joe. They stared at one another, studying each other. It took each only seconds to answer the decades-old question of whether she was his daughter.

Chapter 32

BIANCA CLOSED THE front door when Isabella's driver drove off with Joe and Toni in the back seat.

Bianca threaded her hand through her mother's elbow and led her to the kitchen. "Since you're spending the night, you and I will treat ourselves to a very large, fattening bowl of our favourite ice cream before heading to bed." Bianca held up the container of pralines and cream ice cream she retrieved from the freezer.

"That sounds like an excellent plan." Isabella walked to the white marble-top kitchen island and sat on a stool.

The kitchen was modern, with indigo lacquer cabinets and cream countertops. It had an embedded eight-burner gas stove and a double glass-door refrigerator. The tiles were tan and shiny.

"Toni looked drained and happy at the same time." Bianca fished two spoons and the ice cream scoop from the cutlery drawer.

"She did look shattered, not that I blame her. Finding out about a father you knew nothing about and the family he brings with him is a lot to take in all at once." Isabella watched Bianca reach into the cupboard for two bowls.

The kitchen smelled of Pine-Sol with the lingering smell of dinner: spaghetti with tomato sauce and garlic bread was on the menu tonight—Serena and Rosanna's favourite.

"Agreed, but I think it's the stability she needs. At least, I hope so. She's the best assistant I've had, and I want her back. Besides, she needs to finish what she started with Ming and her team, but I'm sure as hell not taking her back if she doesn't get her shit together."

"I have a feeling she will, as you so eloquently put it, 'get her shit together' once she gets to know her new family. They will give her the love and family life she has lacked all these years," Isabella said, and the smirk twisted Bianca's lips. "Being around positive influences shapes you into a better person. Tonight, they're staying at the corporate house downtown. It'll be a bit crowded, but I think togetherness may be what Toni needs. Tomorrow, they leave on the company jet for the Bahamas. I told Joe they could stay as long as they wanted at our villa to get to know one another. Sun, beach, and piña coladas are the perfect therapy for the broken soul."

"I can't argue with that. Before I go to bed tonight, I'll email the villa staff to confirm their arrival tomorrow." Bianca slid the bowl with three scoops of ice cream and a spoon across the counter to Isabella.

"Hopefully, by the end of their stay, being around all that family, Toni will sort her head out and decide her next step." Isabella scooped ice cream onto her spoon and savoured it.

"Will you tell Dad and Christian all, or do you want me to?" Bianca sat on the stool beside her mother.

"Tomorrow, after the Saturday family lunch, you and I will tell them everything. Christian must know you've done everything possible to help Toni sort things out." Isabella let the next spoonful of ice cream melt in her mouth. Pralines and cream ice cream was good for the soul. "I can only imagine what Michaela has asked of that girl. I can wring Michaela's neck without any remorse."

Bianca's eyes fixed on Isabella. "We've gone above and beyond, Mom. Fingers crossed it works out for everyone because Dad won't be happy with Joe coming into our lives." Bianca brought a spoonful of ice cream to her mouth

"No, he won't." Isabella could already hear Antonio's oath-laced rant, not to mention her mother's and father's. "But he'll have to deal with it. It's what needed to be done for his son's happiness, and your father knows well I'd meet with the devil in a dark alley if it benefitted any of you."

Bianca smiled at her mother, fully aware of the lengths she would go to for the people she loved. "Well, right or wrong, Dad won't be happy. Still, Joe doesn't seem to be the Luciferish type to me. Joe appears to be rather, shall I say it, a respectable man. I can see why you forgave him. Most men would think hard about welcoming a broken child into their life, family, and home. Many would walk away. But Joe didn't think twice about it. He immediately hopped on a flight to meet his long-lost daughter and welcomed her with open arms. That tells me he's an honourable man deserving of respect."

Isabella nodded in implicit agreement. "Circumstances do make the person. It's good that Joe got out from under Michaela when he did. Otherwise, I can't imagine where he would be today or what he'd be doing if he hadn't."

Thoughtfully, Bianca licked her spoon clean. "Makes you wonder what drives people like Michaela and Bob Klein to commit the evil they perpetrate."

"Yes, it does." Isabella scooped ice cream. "Luckily, a greater number of people lean toward the good. And then there's the next generation of women like you who persevere and right wrongs. It makes me believe I'm leaving this world in good hands."

Rosanna and Susanna were in bed, and the house was asleep, and for a moment, Bianca and Isabella sat wordlessly, lost in their thoughts. The clinking of their spoons against bowls and the hum of the refrigerator's motor was noticeable and loud in the quiet. In the distance, a fox howled under the moon's light, and others joined him.

"Joe's not my father," Bianca said quickly and swiftly, like ripping a Band-Aid off.

If the statement rattled Isabella, she didn't let it show. "You sound sure of yourself."

"I am. I sensed it the minute I shook Joe's hand. There wasn't an emotional connection, you know? Like the one I feel with Daddy."

An instantaneous warmth came over Isabella, and she broke into a wide smile. There was no feeling like the connection of a child who was a part of you. "You're right. He's not your father."

Bianca leaned back in her seat and gazed at her mother. "You sound sure of yourself."

"I am." Isabella squeezed her daughter's hand. "I read the DNA report I did on you and Joe before I shredded it. It confirmed you were Antonio's daughter through and through. His blood flows in you, and his DNA makes you who you are."

"I knew it. I always knew it." Bianca sprang to her feet and threw her arms around her mother. "Why didn't you say something before?"

"You never asked after we moved on from that sordid time, and I didn't want to bring it up if I didn't have to."

Isabella hesitated, staring at her daughter. "Oh, honey, I'm sorry. Has this been haunting you all this time?"

"Haunting isn't the right word. I'd say more of a…." Bianca searched thoughtfully for the proper description. "Remote notion in the back of my mind."

"I'm sorry, baby. I should have told you, but I thought, like me, you wanted to put that dark memory behind you."

"Don't do that, Mom. Don't blame yourself for something you didn't instigate and had no control over." Bianca mollified her mother. "We can't control some things, but we can triumph over them. We're Farfalla women made of sturdy stuff. We persevere no matter the obstacles set before us."

Isabella's hazel eyes brimmed with a teary smile. "We are all that."

"Now, finish your ice cream and go straight to bed, young lady. We must recharge our minds and bodies to face Daddy and Christian tomorrow. I suspect illuminating them of what we've been up to tonight will sap our energy."

Chapter 33

THE CONVERSATION WITH Antonio went as badly as expected. Antonio was shocked, outraged, and as cross as he had ever been with Isabella for bringing Joe into their daughter's home and life. Antonio's anger was amplified when Isabella told him she brought the man who assaulted her and did the unspeakable into their lives to benefit Christian's love life.

"Christian's a grown man, not your baby anymore, Isabella. He doesn't need his mother meddling in his love life. He could have dealt with Toni himself," Antonio barked loud enough that Bianca thought his voice would shatter the windows of her living room.

As cross as Maria was with Isabella's chivalrous actions, Maria was a mother first and understood her daughter's motivation. Sal, however, sided with Antonio and joined in his rant.

As mindful as Christian was of Isabella's sacrifice and the risk his sister took, he was happy they had. With their interference, he would be able to reach out to Toni. Christian hoped it was all for naught and Toni would return to him because he was set on marrying her.

Two weeks after their talk, although Antonio's anger had waned some, Isabella decided, for his peace of mind, not to tell him about Joe and his family staying at their Bahamian villa for another week. Sometimes, silence in a marriage was a necessary evil.

One positive outcome of Bianca and Isabella's orchestrated meeting with Joe was that once he told Toni what Michaela did to him and Isabella, Toni's seething anger drove her to retaliate against her mother. Toni had Ming post Michaela's undoctored video of her and Bob Klein online, which she found where her mother would stash it—at their bank's safety deposit box.

In the original video, Bob, not Lorenzo, thanked Michaela for providing the names of the whores while admitting he sexually assaulted them as he ran his hand up between her thighs. In the video, Michaela responds with a smile and opens her legs wider for Bob. Bob smiles and tells Michaela he will be piling on the lawsuits against the women for defamation until he has stripped them of every last dime they own. Running his finger higher on her thigh, Bob proudly gloats about exposing them for the goddamn whores they are.

"They wanted it as much as you do right now," Bob says

Michaela followed Bob's comment with a snorted laugh. "Were any of them as good as I am, baby?"

Bob responds. "No one is as good as you are, sweetheart."

Michaela then asks Bob when she could expect his payment for her services.

The undoctored video went viral, giving Bianca the ammunition to shut down Bob Klein's lawsuit and bring the deserved vindication to the women he affected.

Sitting in Bianca's office, at the guest chair across her desk, Bob Klein straightened in his seat. Deep-rooted shock registered on his face when Bianca told Bob not only would he stop his attack on the women, but he'd end his lawsuit against them, her, and the Farfalla Corporation.

Hot rage burning in Bob, he barked, "I will do no such thing."

Bianca settled deeper in her chair and crossed her slender legs gracefully. "Oh, but you will, Bob, and end it all now."

"Not as long as you refuse to pay my bonus," Bob said confidently and arrogantly.

Eyes levelled on Bob, Bianca opened her laptop and set the video to play. "See that, Bob. It's you."

"It is not." His tone was indignant as his wide eyes watched the undoctored video play on the laptop screen. "How did you get that video?"

"I found it on the internet. You're quite popular. You've racked up over one million views so far and counting."

The revelation stole his breath. "That's a … a deepfake."

"I'm impressed you're familiar with the term. It had to be explained to me. But no, Bob, it's not a deepfake. The one you, or should I say Michaela—" Bianca watched the shock fly into Bob's eyes at the mention of Michaela's name. Bianca continued. "The video Michaela put out of my husband on your behalf was the deepfake. This, you see here, is the original video. The one you had dropped off at my reception was a doctored video."

Bob's spine stiffened. "I don't know what you're talking about."

"Denial is no longer going to help you, Bob. I have a good friend at the U of T computer sciences department, a world-renowned deepfake expert who confirmed it and will testify in court. Only if necessary, of course."

Bianca's hands tented under her chin as Bob sucked in air and hissed it out.

"Jesus fucking Christ, Bianca, I had nothing to do with this." Bob propelled from his chair to pace the office.

Bianca's brow rose. The deluded fool let his tiny brain below take over his reasoning. "You had everything to do with the video."

"I have bills to pay." Bob paced the office while swearing under his breath.

"This ends now, Bob." Bianca slid a file across the desk to Bob. "My legal team drafted that. It states that you will stop your suit against the women and accusing and harassing them. That applies to the company and me, too. It also states you agree to forfeit your bonus and that the Farfalla Corporation will use it as financial compensation for the women whose lives you impacted by your despicable actions. You also agree the balance, if there is any, will be donated to the Farfalla Foundation, which will disperse the funds to women's causes of their choosing."

Bob's reaction was an alarmed one. "I will do no such goddamn thing. Did you not hear what I said? If not, look at the words coming out of my mouth. I have bills to pay."

Bianca watched him pace back and forth with anxious energy. "Carve a path on my office floor if you like, but in the end, you will sign this document." Bianca rolled her Mont Blanc pen toward the file. "Sign, Bob. Now. Or I will sue you to oblivion, and you know I have loads more money than you. I can afford to keep your lawyer tied up in court, racking billable hours until you're bankrupted." Bianca's tone was fierce, and her laser-focused eyes burned into him.

Reluctantly, Bob picked up the pen and signed. Afterward, with one last stare blazing with pure anger, he stormed out of Bianca's office.

Sex was great, but it would never top the high Bianca derived from taking down an entitled prick like Bob Klein.

Chapter 34

TONI DIDN'T RETURN to Toronto, and she didn't contact Christian. Meeting her father and family changed Toni's existence. Toni had a new lease on life and was determined to tuck the past away and move on with her new life, even if it meant leaving Christian behind.

After Toni told Joe some—she wasn't ready to say all—of her sordid life, he felt the fierce fatherly compulsion to protect and shield her from Michaela. Joe talked Toni into returning to Milan with him and her newfound family.

Michaela would never manipulate or exploit Toni again.

Toni's stay at her father's home, a renovated deconsecrated church with lots of stained-glass windows on a sprawling estate fringed with colourful gardens, had her settling into the life she had dreamed about. It wasn't the exciting jet-set life Toni was used to. It was a mundane life of routine, chores, and schedules. It was breakfasts, lunches, and dinners with family around the dining room table.

It was the stability Toni craved.

Toni happily volunteered to take on the daily visits to the open market to shop for the family's meals. Toni did the laundry and housekeeping because with the ordinary tasks came the marvel of laughter, sibling teasing, children running about, the sense of family, and love, so much love—everything that until now had not touched Toni's life.

Toni's new life was now more perfect than she imagined, and she refused to spoil it by taking her mother's calls. The prospect of cutting her mother from her life wasn't easy, but Toni decided it was best for her state of mind.

Some things cannot be forgiven, and Michaela's actions and words were impossible to forget.

With Michaela out of Toni's life, a remarkable calm came over her, and Toni's anxiety lifted. Toni took up painting and spent hours in the garden with Francesca, an avid painter. Toni found she had a talent for putting colour to the canvas.

Toni played piano with her talented sister Aurora and learned the classical compositions of Mozart, Beethoven, and Bach. She happily babysat her niece and nephews because she wanted to spend time with them. With her playboy brother, Massimo, Toni went to bars, danced the night away, and was introduced to like-minded people her age.

Nightly dinners with the family at the dining room table were a must. Otherwise, there was hell to pay with Francesca. Afterward, with the family gathered in the living room for coffee and dessert, Toni played the piano every chance she got.

For the first time, Toni experienced average life and liked it.

"You play beautifully, Toni." Joe looked into the clear blue eyes, filled with happiness and confidence. "Are you enjoying your life here, Toni?"

"I am, very much. Thank you for giving me this." Toni looked around the room at her family, laughing and watching Massimo beat Matteo on the PlayStation while the children cheered.

"I wish I could have given it to you sooner."

"Better late than never."

"Yes. Let's go for a walk, honey. I want to talk to you." Joe put out the crook of his arm.

With some trepidation, Toni linked her arm through his. "Is everything all right? Have I done anything wrong?"

"No, honey, you've done nothing wrong." Joe led Toni outside to the stone bench under the olive tree.

The night air was perfumed with the sweet scents of the garden. A warm breeze fluttered in the air, carrying the steady music of the crickets, cicadas, and croaking frogs. Above, the moon sailed white, its glow sharp in the dark sky sprinkled with glowing stars.

"Isabella and Bianca called today to see how you're doing." Joe waved Toni to sit on the bench as he reached into his jacket pocket for the pack of cigarettes.

"That was nice of them." Toni sat. "Considering."

"It was, and they're smart women who see beyond the surface," Joe said, referencing her disloyalty.

Joe shook one cigarette halfway out of the pack and offered it to Toni. Toni turned it down.

"You would be smart to quit the nasty habit. I want the father I found around for a long while."

"Don't you start, too? I already have three harping women in the house who've taken up the cause of separating me from my only vice." Joe lit the cigarette, inhaled, and let the smoke out slowly.

"Well, now you have four."

"Anyway, Isabella is concerned about you, and Bianca said your job is there if you want it."

Toni felt her stomach lurch. "You want me to leave?"

Joe rested his hand on Toni's shoulder. "No, honey, I don't want you to leave. This is your home now and forever, and you're welcome to stay for as long as you want. I like you being here. We all like you being here."

Toni looked at Joe, her expression unmistakably hopeful. "Do you mean it?"

Joe sat beside Toni and touched her cheek with the loving touch of a father. "Of course I do. We're your family, and you're stuck with us. But you also have your own life to make." Joe blew out a plume of smoke. "Christian sends his love and wants to talk to you."

Toni's stomach pitched. "No. No, I cannot. If Christian knew everything about me, he…. I am so ashamed I have not told you all I have done. I am not ready to tell you everything, let alone Christian." Toni confided. "And what I did to him— No. No, I cannot look him in the eye and tell the man who has picked me up out of the darkness and brought me into his bright light what I have done."

"If he loves you as much as he says, he will overlook your past to build a future with you." Joe watched her brows knit in doubt. "Remember, I was in a position similar to yours with Francesca. Look at us now." Joe rose, tossed the cigarette down, and heeled it out. "It's your decision, honey. I will support you in any decision you decide to make. Just make sure whatever you decide, you don't end up living a life of regret. Promise me you'll think about it. Talk to Aurora and Mia. God knows they have something to say about everything," Joe said with a grin.

AURORA AND MIA HAD A LOT to say. A lot. In the end, both encouraged Toni to hear Christian out. A good man was hard to find, and after they saw his picture on the company's website, they pressed Toni harder to meet with him.

"*Mamma Mia*! You cannot let him go if he looks as good naked as fully dressed." Aurora's eyes remained peeled on Christian's image on the screen.

"The deep blush on Toni's cheeks says it all." Mia laughed and elbowed Aurora in the ribs. "I know I am married to your brother, but I can still think in here," Mia pressed a finger to her head, "what I could do with that."

Aurora snorted a laugh. "You may think that, and I will say, ditto. Does he have long fingers?" Aurora's inquisitive eyes looked away from the screen to Toni.

The pink blush that filled Toni's neck and cheek answered their question. Aurora elbowed Mia as both women gazed at each other knowingly.

The sisterly teasing gave Toni a feeling of inclusivity and put a smile on her face and heart. "It is true what they say about women being worse than men when it comes to gossiping about sex."

"Pfft, yeah. We are way worse." Aurora fell back on the living room sofa and stretched her legs on the coffee table. "But in all seriousness, Toni, you must talk to Christian."

Warming her hands on the coffee mug, Toni said, "I do not know."

"Do you love him?" Mia asked, and both women turned their eyes to Toni and waited for her response.

Without hesitation, Toni said, "I do," and left her thoughts to drift to Christian.

Epilogue

THE MORNING SUN sparkled brightly over Milan.

The piazza teemed with tourists, cameras at the ready, who streamed along, enjoying the sights. Flocks of cooing pigeons, their heads bobbing, moved amongst the crowds, hopeful for food scraps. The shops and boutiques bordering the piazza were crowded with customers buying Italian-made leather and designer clothes branded with renowned names and souvenirs for bragging rights. Café patios were thick with people sipping espresso and cappuccinos and savouring delicious pastries.

Amid the crowded piazza, Christian sat on the fountain's edge, spilling water from the four lion's mouths. Christian rechecked his wristwatch and looked up and all around him. Bianca was fifteen minutes late. Scanning the thronged piazza for his sister, Christian thought he saw Toni.

Christian's heart fluttered like a hummingbird's wings, fast and steady.

Christian was sure he could smell her perfume among the hundreds of people. An excited sigh escaped him as the spear of hope sliced through him.

It had been months since Christian last saw or talked to Toni, and the ache of loss was immeasurable.

Bianca and Isabella told Christian that Toni needed time and space to sort things out and spend time with her newfound family. Christian, however, was running short of hope of seeing Toni again. And here Toni was.

Propelling to his feet, Christian chased after the woman he believed to be Toni but maintained some distance between them. Watching her intently to determine if it was her.

It was her gait, the sway of her hips. It was Toni, he told himself.

In his gut, Christian sensed it was Toni. She wore skinny jeans and a lilac blouse tucked in the front and flowing in the back. She had on tan Roman sandals and a matching cross-body handbag. She carried a canvas shopping bag in her right hand, and the warm breeze that stirred whiffled through her lustrous blonde hair.

Christian saw the peanut vendor flash her a toothless grin on her approach. After a brief chat, he filled a bag with roasted peanuts and gave it to her, waving his hand to turn down payment when she reached into her handbag.

Christian wanted to touch her, just his fingertips on her face, something to smooth away the hurt he carried with him, but he continued to watch her.

Christian watched her wave at several people as she walked past them. He surmised she'd made friends since moving to Milan with her father. She looked happy.

Eyes focused on Toni, Christian followed her as she walked to the market. Her first stop was the fruit and vegetable stand. Greeting the vendor, she picked up an orange and breathed in its scent. She repeated the motion with the lemons and tomatoes and handed them to the vendor for bagging. Toni selected a head of lettuce, onions, and garlic. She paid for her purchase, moved on to the fish and wine stalls, and carefully chose her acquisition.

Toni had made a life here with good friends and family. The heartache pressed down into Christian's chest and cut off his air.

Toni was happy, and Christian began to doubt himself.

Christian fell in love with Toni the moment he met her, but coming to Milan to look for her wasn't the right move. Christian shouldn't have listened to Bianca and made the trip even if she assured him Toni's sister and sister-in-law believed he should.

Unexpectedly and against his will, Christian turned to walk away from the shadows and head back to the family villa. Tomorrow, he'd fly back home and forget Toni.

"You weren't at the meeting spot. You've kept me waiting for fifteen minutes." Bianca appeared from nowhere to block Christian's view.

Bianca looked comfortable and summery in a canary-yellow chiffon dress with a wide skirt and short sleeves. She wore patent flats, and her hair spilled beneath the wide-brimmed hat with a yellow ribbon.

Bianca's comment caused Christian to lift a brow. Pointing out the irony of her statement would fall on deaf ears. "I thought I saw Toni."

Bianca's eyebrows lifted in an expression of interest. "You thought?"

"Yeah, I couldn't bring myself to talk to her," Christian said in a pained voice. "But I followed her, and now she's disappeared into the crowd."

"How do you know it was her if you didn't talk to her?"

"I'd know her anywhere. She appeared happy, settled in her new life. I couldn't talk to her for fear of what she might say." And he'd lost his chance now. "She's happy here, Bianca. She has her family and made friends. She won't return with me, and I can't pull her away from her support system and comfort zone." Christian gave Bianca a look of obvious misery.

Bianca linked her arm through his. "Let's get you a drink, baby brother."

"No. I want to get back to the villa."

Bianca tugged at Christian's arm when he moved to walk away. "It's a perfect day to sit on a patio instead of wasting it indoors brooding. Come on, a quick one." Bianca made her best attempt to move him along.

"Fine, but it will be a quick one. I don't want to be out here longer than I need to be. I'm not good company."

"I promise it will be short. I'm meeting Uncle Carlo in thirty minutes at his nearby store. Let's get a table at the Milano Café."

"It's packed, Bianca," Christian said as they approached the café and saw the packed patio tables and the long line of people waiting to be seated. "We won't get a table for another hour."

"No worries. Friends of mine are holding the table for us. There they are." Bianca pointed to the dark-haired woman with a bright smile who waved at her.

"I'm not in the mood for people, Bianca." Christian turned to walk away, but Bianca blocked him.

"We're here now, and I want you to meet them."

Aurora and Mia rose. Aurora wore slim pants with flats and a flowery blouse open at the neck. Her straight, jet-black hair fell around her heart-shaped face. Mia was petite, inches shorter than Aurora, and had a delicate face. Her hair was as dark and straight as Aurora's.

Aurora and Mia's dark eyes locked on the tall man with tight-fitting jeans, a white shirt tracing muscular arms, and flowing hair framing a tanned face.

Aurora gave an inaudible sigh. "*Gesù*! He is yummy. Better looking in person than on the screen."

Mia concurred with a vigorous nod.

"Who is yummy?" Toni swivelled in her chair to look behind her.

Awestruck, Toni let out a flat-sounding rush of air.

Christian's eyes locked on Toni's and abruptly stopped on the spot. It was her.

Toni's heart throbbed and echoed in her ear as the charge of emotion hit as hard as it did Christian. Motionless and breathless, Toni stared at Christian, and he stared at her.

There was a long, frozen silence. Aurora, Mia, and Bianca looked from Toni to Christian and back to Toni.

"Hello, Toni." Bianca turned her attention to Aurora and Mia when Toni's stunned eyes stayed fixed on Christian. "Hi, nice to finally meet you." Bianca put out her hand.

Aurora met Bianca's hand. "I am Aurora, and this is my sister-in-law Mia."

"It's Nice to put a face to the voice, and thank you for the call and helping me put this meeting together," Bianca said.

"You set this up?" Christian's square, handsome face set in serious lines when he looked at Bianca.

Bianca nodded. "With their help."

Mia and Aurora's eyes sparkled with luminous smiles.

"I am Aurora, Toni's sister, and this is our sister-in-law, Mia." Aurora held out a small, firm hand for Christian's. "We three believe the two of you need to talk." Aurora held Christian's hand tightly and guided him to the chair at the table beside Toni.

"So sit and talk." Mia shouldered her handbag and handed Aurora hers.

"*Andiamo*, Mia." Aurora linked her arm through Bianca's. "So, tell me, Bianca, since we are likely to become family, does it mean we get your clothes wholesale?"

Negotiating was in the Italian genes, Bianca thought. "I may be able to do better than wholesale."

Aurora and Mia's faces went brilliant with pleasure.

"Is your husband Lorenzo with you? I'd love to meet him." Aurora gave Bianca a wink.

Bianca pursed her lips a little. "I thought you were married?"

"I am. I love my husband, and he is gorgeous, but it does not mean I am blind or dead." Aurora snorted a laugh, and Bianca and Mia joined in.

"I'm on my way to Uncle Carlo's store. Would you like to meet him?"

"Yes, we both do." Mia linked her arm with Bianca's free arm.

"*Andiamo*. Lead the way," Aurora said.

"Do you think I can hit him for a discount as well? I love everything Mesi as much as I do Farfalla. By the way, I love your dress. Is it Mesi or Farfalla?" Aurora prattled on as they walked away.

"Is she always that chatty?" Christian asked to fill the lingering silence.

Toni nodded.

"You look great."

"You too." Toni's voice was barely audible.

Christian went silent as the waiter approached the table to check on them. When the waiter retreated to get the two coffees Christian ordered, he said, "It's great to see you, Toni."

Toni said nothing.

"You seem … happy."

Silence.

"I've missed you, Toni. I've missed you so much."

Tears started down Toni's face.

"Please don't cry. I didn't mean to make you cry. I'll go if it's what you want me to do."

Silence.

Christian started to rise but wished Toni would stop him.

"I do not want you to go," Toni said, stopping Christian from taking another step. I have missed you, too."

Christian's joy at the words was evident in his face. "In the months you've been gone, I've realized I don't want to live without you. I can't. I want you in my life. I love you, Toni, and I want to spend the rest of my life with you." The words seemed to hang in the air for a moment.

"I do, too, Christian." Toni leaned across the table and put her hand on Christian's. "But there are things I need to tell you."

"No, you don't." Christian moved to thread his fingers through Toni's and was pleased when she let him. "I've told you I have no interest in your past. I'm only interested in the here and now." He raised their linked hands to his lips.

"No, Christian. I need to tell you. Papa says that a secret could be a very corrosive thing to come between two people. I must tell you everything about me, and you must listen and then decide if you still feel the same way. I will understand if you do not."

Taking a deep breath, Toni told her story from the beginning.

Sneak peek at M.L. Lexi's new novel
THE DETERMINED WOMAN
Prologue

Spring 2007

THAT ONE ACT set everything in motion, and the consequences were still reverberating all these years later. Now, things Isabella thought would remain inside her forever had to be told.

On a long breath, she dropped her weary body into the plush leather of the Kensington recliner. The golden liquid in her glass sloshed dangerously close to the rim. Resting her head against the chair, she squeezed her eyes shut and struggled for calm.

Isabella wasn't under the delusion this moment would never come. She only hoped it wouldn't, but the repercussions of a single vile act could go on and on for years and touch many lives. As hard as Isabella tried to keep the painful experience from reaching her family, the time had come when it would.

Isabella's expression shifted as her daughter's angrily lobbed questions came to her—again.

How could you do this to me, to daddy?

How could you lie all these years, and with such ease, Mother? What else have you been lying about?

Do you know how betrayed and broken I feel knowing the person I love and trust most in this world has lied to me my entire life?

My whole life has been a lie.

The anger hot and pulsing in Bianca's voice as she came at Isabella with the questions, accusations, and hate, her response was to run away—far away from her daughter. Escaping, shrouding herself from everything and everyone was what she needed, and in the darkness of night, Isabella made the two-hour drive to her northern retreat.

No matter how long Isabella had mentally prepared for when the moment came, when it did, it felt like a detonating hand grenade to her system. The shameful, ugly secret she'd kept buried in the deep recesses of her mind for the twenty-three years of her daughter's life, her entire married life now had to be told.

Isabella was bone-tired, but as much as she needed to lay her head down, her racing mind wouldn't allow sleep to come. She did the next best thing. Isabella fueled herself with the remaining brandy in her glass.

Swooping to the bar, she slopped brandy into her glass then crossed to the window. The first light from a rising sun peeked from between the treetops. Isabella cast eyes to the natural, unspoiled surroundings of Lake Rosseau. Spring was beginning to show her face in the small Canadian town, and fields and forests framing the lake were steeped in the budding green heralding the season. Canada geese migrating from their winter sojourn filled a vivid blue sky.

In the deafening silence, her father's words rushed at her.

Secrets are like walls, Isabella. They will protect you and those around you from the pain they can inflict and the harm they can spawn, but only temporarily because no matter how shocking or terrible those secrets are, eventually, they always come out.

Hers now had.

The warmth of the living room suddenly felt stifling, and Isabella stepped out onto the terrace. The air against her face, cool and moist, carried the pungent peaty smell of damp earth and dew from the previous week's rains. The sounds of dawn were all around. Within the shelter of trees that sprang up majestically toward the sky, a soft wind rustled through their leaves. Birds joined in the chorus of birdsong, and creatures stirred.

The soothing and utopian panorama she escaped to when she needed recharging from her busy life today did nothing to calm her restless mind. Today, her heart ached too much. It ached for her daughter and her unsuspecting family. Resurrecting the long-hidden event from her past was going to cause deep hurt.

She prayed her daughter, husband, and son would understand and forgive her. At the thought, they may not, a frightful chill cut deep, and Isabella wrapped her hands around her shivering body.

"How could I have been so careless?" she thought, eyeing the envelope—the cause of all her problems— sitting on the coffee table. Twice she'd attempted to read its contents but hadn't found the courage to do so.

She should have locked the goddamn thing in her office safe when her assistant handed it to her, but there were so many distractions. The ringing telephone, the tantrum from her Vice-President of Sales complaining about late shipments, and her secretary's urging words to get to the boardroom for the meeting she was running late for had her dismissing the envelope. Although Isabella thrived on such chaos, the contents of the envelope, which was about to change her family's life, had her mind distracted, and she rushed off to her meeting, leaving it on her desk for Bianca to find.

Isabella couldn't fault her daughter for the screaming match she'd incited or the accusatory and hurtful words Bianca hurled when she so much as handed her the DNA report she'd requested without her knowledge.

Guilt compressed in a tight ball in the pit of Isabella's stomach.

The should-haves whirled in Isabella's head. She should have done this or that, but it was too little too late, and her impulse was to run to avoid Bianca's demands for answers, for the truth.

Not that she blamed her daughter. If she were in Bianca's shoes, she too would have demanded an explanation, answers. She, also, would have flung the hateful words Bianca hurled like daggers aimed to wound because she and her daughter were alike. The thought, however, didn't lessen the fact Bianca's hurtful words cut Isabella deeply.

You're my mother, the person I trust unconditionally, and now you're nothing but a lying, deceiving— I will never trust you again, Mom, and I couldn't hate you more right now if I wanted to. I hate you. I hate you. I hate you.

Isabella hadn't known a hurt like that of a child telling their mother she hated her.

Her daughter's words echoing in her ears with the intensity they were meant to, Isabella imagined the depth of Bianca's pain, the feeling of betrayal when she read the report.

No one escaped the past, Isabella thought. A shiver cut through her like a serrated knife, and she wrapped her arms around her body for warmth. Closing her eyes, she opened herself to the memories and the lie at the heart of it all.

Coming Soon
The Complete Woman
The Conflicted Woman
The Spiteful Woman
The Tortured Woman

The Relentless Woman Duology
The Relentless Woman
The Vindictive Women

The Unbreakable Woman Trilogy
The Unbreakable Woman
The Brave Woman
The Valiant Woman

Contact us
Email us at mllexiauthor@gmail.com to receive emails whenever M.L. Lexi publishes a new book. There is no charge or obligation and your information will remain confidential.

Visit us at www.mllexi.com to read excerpts of upcoming releases.